Alexander Teetgen

Beethoven's Symphonies Critically Discussed

Alexander Teetgen

Beethoven's Symphonies Critically Discussed

ISBN/EAN: 9783742881700

Manufactured in Europe, USA, Canada, Australia, Japa

Cover: Foto ©Andreas Hilbeck / pixelio.de

Manufactured and distributed by brebook publishing software
(www.brebook.com)

Alexander Teetgen

Beethoven's Symphonies Critically Discussed

BEETHOVEN'S SYMPHONIES

CRITICALLY DISCUSSED

BY

ALEXANDER TEETGEN

With Preface by John Broadhouse

LONDON:

W. REEVES, 83 CHARING CROSS ROAD, W.C.

Dedication.

TO J. O'MABONY, ESQ.

Who taught me, when a happy schoolboy- in the house
of my beloved and venerated master, the Rev. Alfred
Whitehead, M.A., and his dear wife to sing at sight,
who first fostered my passion for music : to that genial
and highly accomplished man, who has vanished from
my view for years, but not from my memory, where he
resides ever, as a kind of Apollo Belvedere of those
far-off days—that New World to which the Columbus,
Man, may never return.

CONTENTS.

PREFACE.

THESE essays originally appeared in *The Musical Standard*, for which paper they were written.

While admitting that the author has at times been carried away by his exuberant fancy, it is impossible to deny that he possesses in a very high degree those powers of analysis without which it is impossible to do justice to, or even approximately to understand, Beethoven. Music is verily the language of the soul —higher, finer, more delicate in its methods, and more ethereal in its results, than anything to which the tongue can give utterance; expressing what speech cannot speak, and affecting, as no mere talking can, the invisible player who manipulates the keyboard of the human intellect, and whom we call *The Soul*. Music is truly of such a nature, and appeals so powerfully and mysteriously to that soul, that the words of Jean Paul seem quite justified,—

Ich glaube, nur Gott versteht unser Musik.

Beethoven wrote such music as few even among those calling themselves musicians can understand, as the word is generally used; and which, in Jean Paul's sense of the word, is understood not at all. Like the ocean, or Mont Blanc, we can feel its power, while at the same time we are conscious that explanation would be almost desecration. We do not want Beethoven's music explained, but would rather be left alone with that which we can only feel, but cannot understand while hampered with "this mortal coil." Under the spell of such music, we can only explain the emotions it produces in us, and we can only do this in a fashion far from complete. Mr. Teetgen has only attempted an explanation of Beethoven's symphonies in this latter sense; and so far from feeling his little book as an impertinence — which any attempt to explain Beethoven's music (his soul, *id est*) would be —we feel helped in our endeavours to understand something of the means by which the greatest tone-poet worked his incantations and wove his spells.

We cannot always agree with Mr. Teetgen in his estimate of other composers—notably, Mendelssohn, whom he holds in much lighter esteem than we do, and we could not endorse all he says of Mozart, either; he does not worship his great hero too much, but the others too little. Of his most intense admiration for Beethoven, however, none can doubt; and those who read this little work will, we think, agree with us in saying that Mr. Teetgen's analytical and descriptive powers, in dealing with the symphonies, are on a par with his veneration for the great master whom we all delight to honour, and who realised his own ideal—some of us, at least, think so—"There is nothing higher than this—to get nearer the Godhead than other men, and thence diffuse its beams over mankind." Fashions change in music as in other things; but Beethoven's music has in it that truth which, being eternal, cannot change; and we cannot conceive a state of culture so advanced that these Symphonies shall be deemed old-fashioned. If ever that condition is reached, it will be reached not by progression, but retrogression.

J. B.

BEETHOVEN'S SYMPHONIES CRITICALLY
AND SYMPATHETICALLY DISCUSSED

BEETHOVEN'S HARBINGERS.

THERE are some words of such indefinite pregnancy that they expand the soul when we pronounce them. The highest of these I do not name; but "love" is one, "spirit" another, "immortality" another, and "symphony" another. We suppose, the first symphony was when "the morning stars shouted together for joy;" and the mystic world-tree, Igdrasil, with its "leaves of human existence," and myriad manifestations, maketh a symphony for ever in the ear of the Eternal. As music is sound, so perhaps all sound is music, to a higher being—even the discord of pain, and the half cadence of sorrow being justified by a soul of meaning; just as music proper, itself would not be half so sweet or complete without its profound minors and expressive dissonances. The world is full of music—from the "tiny-trumpeting gnat" and the forest-buzz of summer, the happy murmur of the sea on its mother's breast, and the equally happy hum of the bee in the waxen cup, to the scream of the eagle and the roar of the lion, the thunder of the breakers and of heaven's artillery. Every one has observed how the very creak of a door may sometimes rise into music. And the whole world goeth up in music, swelling the symphony of the spheres. But, from these ground tones—these universal hints to their human expression and counterpart in the "father of all such as handle the harp and organ," was a long, long way. Nature waited to produce her mouthpiece, Man, to manifest herself forth in that prolongation of herself which we call *human* nature. Then the vague sublimity of unfettered sound became incorporated in tone—became conscious—and spoke more humanly to the soul of man. At length, after a whole history of evolution, the pride of modern times—modern music—appeared ; and in due course, after a tottering infancy and empiric youth, the modern symphony. As in every case, the outcome is the result of an endless series of gradations ; for, if nature abhors a vacuum, she at least equally abhors drawing a line, and taking a jump. Therefore, if we denominate brave old Haydn as the father or founder of the modern symphony, it is for happy convenience sake, and not because strictly accurate. Always there were Agamemnons before Agamemnon ; and Haydn borrowed and imitated like everybody who is first student and then master (in his old age, *sogar*, he learnt of and benefitted by Mozart). Cursorily we may mention as kinds of forerunners Bach's "Suites," such a piece as Purcell's prelude to "King Arthur" (what a prelude would such a subject demand now ! Milton, too, thought of poemizing King Arthur) ; and Handel's "Pastoral Symphony," which so beautifully and for ever corroborates old King George's remark (which we suspect he stole). The value of no word is known till the greatest master of it has arrived. This is strikingly illustrated by a Handel symphony, and a Beethoven. It is the latter which expands the better part of us in the way spoken of at the outset. The unconscious men of Handel's time used it in little more than the sense of a strain; and here it may be remarked that progress is impossible without consciousness, but that—wheel within wheel—the higher consciousness will always have a soul of unconsciousness. The two are *sine quâ non*. Conservatism and convention are the eternal necessary protests and counterpoises to chaos; and *every* man has his *roots* in his time (and in the past); therefore we are not surprised that Haydn constructed his symphonies in the mode and spirit of that day—especially retaining the minuet—which Beethoven himself only later discarded for the scherzo. Moreover, a moment's reflection will show us that the form of a symphony, as of a sonata, is naturally dictated, of inner necessity, by the simple need of natural contrast. An adagio may well open the piece—so may an allegro; but then we certainly want an andante, or largo; scherzo, or minuet, are next expected; and a presto to wind up—for art also is dependent on flesh and blood; and the human body, as well as mind, dictates many of art's proceedings. The form, then, of the symphony was, we may say, on the whole, dictated, from the beginning of things. Nobody can particularly claim to be its inventor; "nature, even in art, has ever the greatest share." If Haydn could really claim to be the inventor of the symphony, he would be a far more original genius than he is ever believed to be—though probably we do really underrate his originality, a fate which inevitably overtakes all such men. If we leave the form, then, and consider the spirit of

Haydn's symphonies, it is, shortly, the spirit of eternal youth; just as one could apply to Mozart Gilfillan's appellation of Shelley, " the eternal child." We get a negative idea of Haydn if we reflect how infinitely removed from Hamlet! (Beethoven, on the contrary, how allied!—a German .Hamlet). I do not believe that Haydn, any more than the other two of that glorious Orion's belt, was a " good Catholic." I imagine, all three had a proclivity rather to natural than revealed religion ; and I believe that we may compass and understand, in a manner, that marvellous outburst of South German music, with all its freedom and glow, by considering it as Roman Catholic without Roman Catholicism ; one feels and sees rather the eternal truth and poetry of nature than the warped narrow spirit and practice, and garish glare, of papal dogma, priest-presided slavery, and superstition. But, to quit these impossible difficulties, the music of all three is stamped by one grand common characteristic — it is German. When to nationality we add individuality, we are more or less near to a tolerable understanding of it. Race is mixed in every man—who can resolve it? The influence of religion—especially so-called religion—is nearly as obscure ; but nationality and individuality we can to some extent comprehend. No better epithets are to be found for Haydn than the time-hononred ones of "genial," "cheerful." We like to think of him under his poor old gable-roof, that let in the rain—happy at his poor old spinnet. Touching picture ! the irrepressible spirit of the obscure composer, miserably poor, and neglected, for the first fifty or sixty years of his life ! But the stars, we know, shone in on him through that dim old gable ; and the grass outside was not fresher in spring than the spirit of Joseph Haydn. If reading, alone,

maketh a "full man," as Bacon says, then Joseph
Haydn was, I imagine, a very empty one. He knew
nothing of books, or society, and little of men ;
direct out of the fulness of his melodious heart he
uttered himself forth in poetic music essentially
genial and vigorous, "spraying over," as our German
cousins say, with kindly humour. A "man child " he
was, who will ever be historically—if not contem-
poraneously—immortal. The great forerunners ! we
owe them a debt which we must at last lose out of
sight ; but verily they *have* their reward ! Haydn's
fundamental simplicity and child-like objectiveness,
utterly prevented him from giving us Beethovenian
music. He neither read, nor thought—nor did he feel
very deeply. The doubts and difficulties which Brendel
finely (though mistakenly, perhaps) speaks of Mozart's
having fought out beforehand unconsciously, Haydn
neither consciously nor unconsciously experienced.
He was simply and purely a German musical genius
of his time, blessed with one of the happiest consti-
tutions ever given to mortal—*mens sana in corpore
sano.* The unfathomable and infinitely involved
beauty of Beethoven's symphonies is not to be dreamt
of in Haydn. Those of the latter, indeed, may smell
at times rather of the peruke than of the lion's mane
(whence what "dew-drops"!) But such melodious
eloquence as Haydn's "Hymn to the Emperor," one
cannot imagine perishing—it is like a rainbow out of
the Eden-time, hung for ever in heaven. The "Creation,' too, is so inexpressibly fresh, naïve, vigorous,
and beautiful, that it has given to some more *pleasure*
than the very "Messiah." "The heavens are tell-
ing," must be surely also melodious eloquence
immortal, with its exquisite opening and noble
culmination. The music of Haydn (Mozart
too) may, perhaps, emphatically be called natural ;

in spite of—especially in the minuets— that *non so che*
which summons up the old-fashioned continental
noblesse and the frigid gardens of Versailles. If we
want a taste of this—or, also, after our higher flights
(and none the less after our intermediate and sub-
terranean flights in the wizard world of a Wagner),
a banquet in the unlaboured loveliness of old time,
we shall recur to Haydn ; but if we want the higher
flights, and broader flights, and deeper flights themselves, the sublime loveliness and Alpine grandeur
—not Saxon Switzerland, but Tell's—we shall hasten
with reverence and gladness to Beethoven, who towers
above Haydn—and also above these colossal upshoots
of this later "tertiary" period ; for these latter men
seem rather intense than universal ; whereof more
anon.   A German word or two (they are always interesting, because earnest,) about Haydn, and we turn
to Mozart.   "Köstlin's remark about Haydn holds
good also for his symphonies :—With Haydn began
the free-style epoch, the spring and golden age of
music.   In him, music became conscious that she
was not system and science, but free motion, and
lyrical."   Free motion—yes, significant words.   What
e.g., would the sea, would light be, without that?
Undulatory free light !   And I had as lief compare
music with light as anything.   As postscript here, we
may recall Haydn's indignant exclamation after a
Dryasdust dictum by the then pedantic oracle, Al-
brechtsberger, respecting, forsooth—I believe—our
old acquaintances, those irrepressible "consecutive
fifths" :—"This will never do" !   exclaimed Haydn ,
"art must be free."   How really curious it is, your
pedant never flashes *such* a glance into things—into
his own trade.   But, indeed, the poor man can never
have a glimmering of what one little word, yet so
multum in parvo, like "free" means.   He is full of

learning, it is true, but still "in block"; and when the Apollo at his side suddenly takes wings, and flashes out of the marble, he knows not, poor man, whether he is more astounded or indignant. A clever man called Shakespeare, also, a barbarian. When will Dryasdust see that, *cœteris paribus*, where innovation is the step of genius, and *not ignorance*, he, Dryasdust, had better, at least for a while, hold his tongue; see, rather, if he can't, by a dead-lift effort, raise himself up to Apollo, than try (ridiculously enough) to drag down the god flashing to the sun. I fear the diffi- culty is insuperable, because subjective. The mis- fortune is, Dryasdust never *can* recognize genius, but wanders on with his blue "specs." to his unvisited grave.

But, to recur to Elterlein, *ueber* Haydn :—" When we look into Haydn's symphonies a little closer, with a glance at the same time at Haydn's followers, we find them stamped by greater simplicity in the expres- sion of feeling, and by a limitation to certain well- defined spheres of mood and humour. This charac- teristic we may express in the definition, pure child- like ideality. Of course, we do not mean literal childhood, but rather abstract childhood in the soul and constitution, whose representation is worthy of the greatest of artists, *e.g.*, of a Schumann in his charming 'Kinderscenen.' Naïve child humour plays a leading part in Haydn's symphonies; where- fore Brendel rightly names him the greatest master of sport and mood. Of inner necessity, the pangs and earnest of life, in their entirety, are excluded from these works. They do now and then appear, but only as light clouds skimming over. Haydn's restrict- edness is, however, far from limiting his invention; on the contrary, we are astounded at it; he is veri- tably inexhaustible in his mode of expressing himself. The minuets are generally playgrounds for the most delicious sportive humour. (In Haydn himself we discover the germs of the so-called programme music :—*e.g.*, symphonies entitled 'The Bear,' 'Maria Theresa,' 'The Schoolmaster'). We now turn to Mozart.

Mozart was a world's-wonder in his boyhood, and neglected—especially at Vienna, and by the court—in his manhood. He has been denominated the most abstract musician that ever lived—a term which is more or less suggestive, if not precise. But, in so far as it points to his being wholly and solely a musician, it points to a defect and hindrance in him. (It has been said, however, that he had a great aptitude also for figures, and would have made no contemptible mathematician. His parents were one of the hard-somest couples of their day.) Robert Schumann's wonderful music, so rich in contents (*inhaltreich*), sprang from a cultivated poet, equally practised with the heart, and soul, and brain, and hand. Wagner's marvellous art is the birth of a similar genius. In short, the age we live in has certainly this advantage : an artist now must be an educated man (in many senses). Haydn and Mozart—who never found time for study—were ill-informed, nay, ignorant men. They knew nothing of the past, little of the present, and less than nothing of the future. Beethoven, I think, certainly did know more—if only a little—and compensated for his deficiency by what alone can compensate—overpowering genius, universally colossal. I do not undertake to affirm that greater culture would have improved Haydn and Mozart, but I throw out the suggestion. Possibly, by expanding their minds, and strengthening their faculties, it might have done so. By reading (not only musical) they might have got new lights—loam and enrichment to their own fertile soil; they might have, at least, *widened* that channel of inspiration which they were. A man's utterance, whether it be musical or other, is, at bottom, the outcome of the whole man. I know, that, in literature, such "education" as I have glanced at—a discipline and growth all ways, through *communion* with deeper and higher spirits, and thoughts, and truths, has the effect I speak of. Natural genius is deepened, and enriched, and expanded, and sent up higher; roots and leaves, with increased fruit-capacity, grow together. It may be, therefore, that Haydn and Mozart, *minus* a Shakespeare's genius (which seems an utter self-justified exception), owe their deficiency in music to their deficiency in culture—in a scientifically comprehensive sense. They were *too* much musicians. It may be, that the fact of their lack was partly also due to an original inherent non-proclivity to culture. If so, here we have a deeper explanation; the bare fact is seen to be the symptom of a radical cause. But Beethoven was a born thinker : remember his flashes of remark :—"Read Shakespeare's 'Tempest.' 'So knocketh Fate at the portals.' 'I have another law for myself than Kant's "Categorical Imperative." ' ' Better water from my body than from my pen.' " He was a born thinker; and in this fact we have the deeper explanation of his mighty music. Do we not see the fact stamped on his very brows ! the very thrones of concentrated thought,—as the deep-set eyes full of dusky fire in the lion-like head are the homes of intense feeling, such as, possibly, no man equalled. The comparison, let alone the coupling, of Mozart with Shakespeare, I, for one, cannot for a moment away with ; in fact, am inclined to cry with that author who could not tolerate a similar bracketing of Turner with Shakespeare, "Bah !"

There is a power, a depth, a *seraphic* wisdom of inspiration and universal view, an oracular utterance and constructive power *from within* (the nearest approach to the Divine *modus operandi* itself) in Shakespeare which Mozart can lay no proper claim to. The theory which would make his " Don Juan " characters (forsooth !) display this similar power—in the organic dramatic verisimilitude of the music—I cannot endorse. Only a very long way off is your Mozart like Shakespeare, with whom, properly, no one can measure, or be likened. He stands alone, a phenomenal unique. Such divine propriety he had! the intellect of an archangel; and a prolonged moulding-from-within power from Nature. Mozart had a lovely, sometimes heavenly, profuse—not incontinent—gift of melody, which is wont, however, to tire (unlike Beethoven's), by being too Mozartish ; a marvellous genius for counterpoint ; and a beautiful instinct for harmony and form. He was, *par excellence*, amiable; his music is loveable. He shines like the sun on a mild spring day. That he has serenity, as Shakespeare had, of course is patent and cardinal ; but that it is Shakespeare's serenity I must beg to dispute. Shakespeare's is profound as the centre of the sun ; Mozart's is rather diffusive than profound or moonlike. Shakespeare's is that of a god-like man ; Mozart's that of an " eternal child." Mozart's is that of the Mediterranean ; Shakespeare's of the whole ocean. And of Shakespeare—not of Mozart (according to our instinct)—may it be so eloquently asserted, " his serenity is that of one " (a *Potente*, as Dante says) " who had unconsciously fought out beforehand all the doubts and difficulties, and put them to flight." Mozart is supposed to have been " light o' love," if not fond of wine too. To be

" light o' love " goes very well with the composer of
" Don Juan," but I do not think anybody ever charged
it on the inspirer of the passionate grandeur of the
Countess Guicciardi sonata ; of the heroic, C minor
and other symphonies. *Had* he been so, we should
have had *such* strains of remorse wailing up. Do we
find them in Mozart ? I trow not !—" Thy terrible beauty, Remorse, shining up from the depths of
pain !" Mozart is cheerful, beautiful, at times vigorous ;
but surely somewhat light—a mountain lake with
fleecy clouds, not the sea, with its sunsets and thunders. Not *his* serenity, but Beethoven's rather, pre-
supposes, like the sun of summer, and calm heart of
nature, all the storms fought out (?) Was there, as in
Beethoven, a soul of earnestness in him ? Had he
aim, consciously, or unconsciously ? Does he speak
from inspired depths, almost painful ? Had he a
glimmering of atheism ? Did he ever clutch at the
vanishing skirts of the Almighty ? Could he kill
himself almost, to be sure of immortality ? So far
from thinking he had thought and fought all these
things out, consciously or unconsciously, we feel that
he had no experience of them—*could* not have—and
so was for ever an incomplete man. " He knew not
ye, ye mighty powers." Sunshine he can give us ;
yes, but sunshine *and* thunderglooms (say, tropical)—
roar of ocean, and spasm of lightning—no. His best
symphonies will not strictly compare with Beethoven's
best ; his sonatas still less. And it is no very adven-
turous prediction (however horrifying to sundry), that
his " Don Juan "—" the first opera in the world " (!),
with its contemptible trash for libretto, and meagre
musical constituents, will hide its diminished head more
and more, till it disappear. Mozart, says the German essayist, means operas rather than symphonies :

well, and what did he make of them? At this time
of day, it is simply inconceivable how any intelligent
man—let alone a tone-poet—could set trash by the
hour or week together. It has become almost a trite
idea now, that poetry is the soul of music : *caeteris
paribus*, in proportion as the word is divine, so will
the flesh be, which it takes unto itself and moulds
from within, in which it eventuates. How great by
comparison is Handel here ! We have but to think
of his words—" Hallelujah ! Lord God Omnipotent !
He shall reign for ever and ever, Amen !" to explain
why we may search Mozart in vain for a Hallelujah
Chorus, that temple of immortality ! Beethoven, inde-
finitely higher and greater than Mozart, did have a
notion of the exigency of the word—he spent hours
and hours looking through some hundred libretti for
an opera, and rejected them all. In setting trash,
poor dear Mozart, the gifted, the easy-going nature,
conscious of little but his fluent genius, and thinking of little but winning his painful bread for the
day passing over, did not reflect that he was guilty of
sacriligious high treason ; as it were, of violation of
Pallas Athene herself. " Music !" another of those
infinite words ! When will her servants be worthy of
her ? When will she suffer the veil to be completely
drawn away, and reveal herself in her full beauty ?
Not by the hands of a Mozart, with his deplorable
" Don Juans " and chaotic nonsense of magic flutes.
In his better sacred music he is better. But even in
that I detect neither real belief—which can alone jus-
tify sacred music, and ensure its highest excellence—
nor a great soul. Mozart was an inspired child ;
when grown up, a child-man—as Hadyn was a man-
child. Nature selected him to speak out this element
in her, as she selected Beethoven to speak out her

passion and paradox, her divine and her terrible beauty—her world-wide grandeur—the infinitude of her universe; as she selected Schumann to speak out her romance, and twilight beauty; and Wagner her supernatural, demoniac, wizardlike. We must recollect, too, that Mozart was the child of his time. Every man is this, more or less, *plus* his individuality. Now, in truth, Mozart seems rather "more," not "less." Beethoven approaches Shakespeare, in being for all time; but not Mozart. His individuality was not strong enough. I cannot agree with Elterlein, that Mozart represents " fair, free, humanity," if we are to give a higher, a Shakesperian meaning to these words. Shakespeare was truly representative of the Wisdom, viz., that covers the whole world, and every age; and belongs neither to the past, present, nor future, but to all time—to all three together; and so is the unique shadow afar off in the history of man, of the eternal I Am and Now. But such high language we can by on manner of means apply to Mozart, who hadn't a tithe of Shakespeare's insight and power; nor a third part of Goethe's—with whom Elterlein and others also put him. The " fair, free, humanity," which, in its unfettered action and thought towers towards the divine, which has long ago sloughed away, or stepped out of old crusts and rags of prejudice, superstition, and the things whose name is legion—but which remains equally free from shallow sin and selfish action; from the paralysis of indifferentism, and the laziness of no-thought; from mere bread-winning, and waste of genius (which waste is always rapidly hurried into oblivion)—this " fair, free, humanity," Mozart does not, can not, as it seems to us, represent. Shakes-peare and Goethe truly do. And Beethoven, in his happier, victorious moods—in his darker moods he shadows forth rather man on the way to it; or, indeed, on the way from it. Elterlein couples Mozart with Raphael, as well as Goethe; that may pass; but who can imagine either of the two former being capable of a "Werther" and "Faust"? Mozart may "stand alone" for "amiability," and may truly enjoy the reputation of giving us, more or less, organic form; but he was a limited, local nature, neither based on the lowest deeps nor towering into the highest heights. He was no reformer,—did not revolutionize music (his operas are but German-Italian by an Italian-German, to that extent), no one can call him colossal. He was a palm, rather than an oak. Handel, to me, is a name far grander. Like Beethoven, I would bare my head at *his* tomb. And now let us turn to the shadowy colossus himself—towering aloft

"In stifled splendour and gloom."

If there are some nouns that affect us, there are some proper nouns that equally do so. One of the most potent of these is "Beethoven." At the mere mention of that name, we experience a "shock of joy" and reverence at once vaguely and vastly filling us with the sublime and beautiful—the grand and tender; in short, with all those attributes, in a degree, of Nature, for this seems to be the special and peculiar function and privilege of genius—of great human nature—to reflect and reproduce, with, as before noted, the force and charm peculiar to itself, nature, divinity. Great men are distinguished by the height to which they tower in doing this; they are but further manifestations of God—revelations of arcana. Up to our time, no man in any art has so towered aloft more than Beethoven. Armed with the most mystical of prophecies and utterance—music, he strewed abroad upon the winds and world such pregnant messages as stirred men to depths they were before unconscious of, and live and operate with the force of immortality. Let us approach these wonderful works and glance more or less into their truly divine depths. We shall not, however, by any means be indiscriminate—in the sympathy of the hero-worshipper forget the justice of the judge. We shall not forget that the best of men are but men at best; and that, for our comfort and ensample, as ever, the great Beethoven was also a child, a beginner, a student, an acolyte, as well as imperial master; and, alas! mortal man—with his sad liability to madness and decay; with his basis on the infernal, as well as heights in the divine.

In the first place, what shall we say about the peculiarly original Beethoven's reflection at the outset of Hadyn and Mozart? At first sight, it rather jars. But shall we be correct if after consideration we pronounce that this is rather a merit, and to be expected, than otherwise; for it is characteristic of hero-worship, which is most passionate in genius truly original. Shakespeare, perhaps, is the great or even sole exception; but, as it is borne in on us, Shakespeare seems to be unique—a semi-god, or "seraph," rather than mere man; and I, for one, have no disinclination or repugnance to own that Beethoven, like the rest, does not equal Shakespeare. In parts he does—perhaps even gives us more terribly grand glances into depths than *Macbeth* and *Lear*—but not as a whole. It is the whole of Shakespeare that is so unique and overpowering. Beethoven often suggests rather Dante and Milton; though it is his peculiar praise, too, that he suggests all three, and yet is like none.

And now to work :

SYMPHONY No. 1, Op. 21.

"Opus 21."—So, when Beethoven came of age, musically speaking, he wrote . his first symphony. Ah! who can realize the feelings of a Beethoven sitting down to write his first symphony; *fuller* feelings probably were not, and could not, be in the world, among all the manifestations of human existence. What flush of hope! what throbs of pleasure! what high-beating plethora of imaginative blood! what almost painful fulness!—necessity to rush forth in poetic utterance, and fling all together what of latent as well as patent was within him! what struggling consciousness—what waking sense of giant powers—what secret assurance in the end of immortal victory, nay, perhaps, of an empire in music towering aloft above that of Hadyn and Mozart and predecessors and successors of all nations and individualities. I envy neither the powers nor immortality of that contemporary, Napoleon, compared with those of Beethoven :—Meteoric Corsican adventurer—eternal eldest son of genius! Dazzling egotist and semi-quack—concentrated sun of nature and the imperishable heavens!—I wonder what Beethoven had been reading previous to undertaking his first symphony—what he had been doing, talking, thinking! I like to picture imaginary scenes where he sat down to the intoxicating enterprise. Was it in the country, of an early morning, all dripping in the sunshine like the orange-bowers here, with the sun welcoming with his sweetest smile the fleecy clouds wandering up the heaven? Or was it (probably it was, for reality is painfully prosaic,) in some back attic—such as where Shakespeare perhaps wrote *his* symphonies? The sublimely interesting young Beethoven! There he sits for a moment with his two hands pressed on those concentrated brows of the lion-like head, previously to penning the first chord! There he sits—look at him well—the fullest incarnation of music, till now the greatest home, emporium, and royal residence of musical power, with all which that implies—including, lowest down, the ineffable; for, always, a man is tender in proportion as he is strong, great in proportion as he is good—Ludwig van Beethoven, in his divine genius and terrible infliction (one of the most painful ironies of human history—like a fate out of high Greek story), one of the most intensely interesting of the race of men!

And now for our criticism; or, rather, for our impressions—for every one of us is dominated by unknown moods and biasses. And the wise spirit which made Goethe call his autobiography "Fact and Fancy," should rule every critic—often the victim and slave of himself, the child of circumstance and time.

First, for a general remark:—I see no essential difference—query, should there be?—between a symphony, especially a Beethoven one, and a sonata. Next, as corollary, let us even say that some of his sonatas (or at least parts) surpass the symphonies. For instance, that first part of the sonata "Patetica," as it is absurdly called, always impresses me as something really almost colossal—the "grave" itself truly so, like a temple four-square, based on the foundations of the world, and high towering towards all the winds. There is no comparison between it and any of the movements of the "No. 1 Symphony," except the first; and here, too, I am inclined to give the palm to the "Patetica," which, *au reste*, curiously enough is just as incongruously weak in the remaining movements as this symphony. Both, in fact, have one element (or stamp) in common, viz., the energetic, which we may characterise as martial—heroic. Beethoven is peculiarly distinguished by this—*plus* a tender beauty of the most profound and healthy description. It is as with the fascinating Schumann; who is equally conspicuous for the energetic and tender—more mystical than Beethoven's, if not so healthy. But, in spite of the ineffable in Beethoven, I almost think we associate power more peculiarly with him. With power Beethoven ushers in his "No. 1." Mark that sforzando, and—B flat. A similar effect occurs in the opening to "Prometheus" (which we noticed independently of Berlioz). Here Beethoven—young and consciously vigorous—took that step of genius we adverted to as opposed to the rashness of ignorance; as it were, champion king-at-arms, flinging the gage of defiance to all the Dryasdusts alive. Poor Dryasdust! who never can be manly enough or genius enough to get free. Dryasdust, it is well known, armed with his blue "specs" and properly obscured thereby, enounces, pronounces, and proclaims —"Allah Akbar! it is unlawful and forbidden to open with a discord" (just as the poor Midas declares it is unpermissible to end in any other key—what has that got to do with it?). Young Beethoven, however —thank the god of originality—has inspired instinct— says "No," and "Take that! you'll soon get used to it." We do get used to it, and then—O the copyists! That B flat is a stroke of genius. Hence we learn, from what *depths* genius speaks—your Beethoven young and vigorous, fresh into the world, henceforth to be a lawgiver and creator of the imperishable. That "B flat" is power; in short, all that originality includes and implies. But, to pass on from this point, which—as every point—might furnish an essay. The *p* after the *sf* is noteworthy ; so, too, the chords —powerfully beautiful, unexpected. The strain is not peculiarly Beethoven ; it does give us a taste of that Ineffable in him, but is meagrely brief—in fact, fragmentary and uncharacteristic—besides, too much suggesting " Prometheus." *Re* the latter, a word *en parenthèse.* After hearing it, Haydn met Beethoven and complimented him on it. " Yes," said the young giant, " but it does not equal the ' Creation ' ". " No, I don't think it quite does," was the reply from the old maestro, " who didn't seem to like the remark." Poor, dear old Haydn ! the glimmering suspicion he had was true enough—that young giant would shake dew-drops from the lion's mane more precious than the grandest Louis Quatorze peruke, plus the unspeakable Louis himself—sarcasm apart, would infallibly eclipse even Haydn's " Creation," naïve and fresh as that may be. We approach the " Allegro " *con amore.* It stirs our depths ; it fills us with ideas. *En passant*, it opens with the same notes of the Sonata in F, Op. 54 (I think). This is another proof that it is not quite true that even Beethoven " never repeats himself;" though it is perhaps true enough to be said—because characteristic ; and when he repeats himself, he generally does so consciously—the great point (another text for essay). The *p* on the chord C E G rather surprises us—we expect a forte (?)—but it has original beauty, and makes an harmonious breathing instead of an emphatic utterance. The following, in the bass, is equally characteristic. As it goes on, the passage is powerfully suggestive, especially at the *cresc.* in unison. The mind's-eye sees a great river rising to overflow its mountain-guarded banks ; or, forsooth, a great nation, to guard them ! All this is the early

Beethoven almost at his best—a true foreshadower of *the* Beethoven—as much as to say, I *am* Beethoven, in spite of Haydn, my very good master, and Mozart. We see the giant waking. About the next *motiv* I hardly know what to say. In one mood it strikes me, like many other things even in Beethoven, as an incongruity; I think, "Why all at once this pastoral strain in the middle of a warlike defiance!" Such unconsciousness as this is an error. A genius must be an artist as well; and a man has no right to fling the first idea that occurs to him into a piece, which is incongruous with the whole. Undoubtedly Beethoven himself sinned here, and not seldom. It is notorious that he tacked on and foisted in pieces which literally had nothing to do with the work as a whole. Lazy or even thoughtless bad taste is a high crime in art —for art truly means, tasteful industry. The sense of fitness must not be offended. Incongruity is a great fault. The men of the conscious school are right here. Consciousness truly has its duties as well as its dangerous frailty. So we argue in that mood. But yet again, so diversified is music, we feel a peculiar, almost unspeakable charm, when, sympathetic fancy coming to our assistance, we consider this abstractly beautiful strain as giving us a glance back from the press of warriors and the noise of battle, to the green fields and silver streams far off we have left; and we think of Arnold von Winkelried leaving his wife and children, as in Deschwanden's affecting picture, so familiar in Switzerland. Then, almost tears come into the eyes, and we exclaim—Oh! thou unconscious wizard, Beethoven!—making us give to thy utterances a meaning thou thyself never didst dream of. Soon again, after this wistful glance back— with none of the sin in it of

Lot's wife—we have the thunder and blaze of war, with his pride, pomp, and circumstance. Nay, I will say, arc we not even reminded of the world-famous Symphony, No. 8, itself? Have we not essentially the same clamour and glamour? our blood is roused, hearts beat high, and we feel we are on the road to righteous victory—"Against the tyrant fought with holy glee." The *pp* strain ensuing does not strike as incongruous, but of peculiar feeling and beauty. How beautifully melody, harmony, and bass, are all one—work together for good, and progress to the climax. As a bit of writing, it is a model for study ; a very charming instance of the success of true scholarship and feeling—scholarship based on feeling ; scholarship unconscious, so that the effect is nature. The codetta carries us back again to the pastoral mood—whence we are congruously re-taken to the warlike by the pompous vague chords—long used before Stephen Heller, for instance !—at the end.

Part No. 2 suggests at the outset one broad general remark, which we hasten to make. It is this. Beethoven, herein not original, but imitative, generally confines himself—in the sonatas as well—to making the second part mostly a mere elaboration of the first. Now, we beg—at all events, at this time of day—to dissent from, and traverse this. We are for making your first part long enough, and repeating it if you will ; but for giving us mostly new ideas, yet in character, in the second. We are not afraid of the "as a whole" theory ; *da capo* we traverse the dogma that what you have got to do is, to give one good idea thoroughly worked out. Wagner has carried this to a wearisome excess. We want no opera or symphony constructed out of "four notes" or forty.

We want not an idea, but ideas. Your vaunted elaboration does not disguise—or rather conceal—the essential sameness—which becomes tameness. And we don't want as sets-off mere "episodes." Beethoven's episodes, as here, are of course, interesting; but, because episodes (?) fragmentary, intercalated, rather than essential; postponements of the old "Hauptsache," rather than independent new ideas. Because this second part is essentially but an elaboration (often a mere repetition, in another key, of ideas already repeated—surely, for the most part, an exploded error?), we have little new to say. The harmonious progressions to the episodes will be studied and felt by every musician. The minor passage, la—do—mi—sol nat.—la, is fine, but not novel in Beethoven. The crash, *ff*, is characteristically grand; the whole elaboration full again of power—power that *is*, and prophetic power to do; power latent and patent. At the beautiful contrapuntal passage in E flat we are again reminded of the F Sonata. The melodious breathings—which must be studied—a little farther on, teach us the very beautiful and interesting lesson (another subject for essay) of the unconscious effect of imitation; and of the unconscious imitation which often lies in effect. The progressions and culminations are Beethovenially grand; in fact, the whole second part superior, if possible, to the first, once admitted the right or propriety of the *modus operandi*. As a whole, the movement stands four-square, noble, filling us with the benefit and pleasure of energetic beauty. This is life—*mens sana in corpore sano;* no hint or shadow of madness; youthful power, generosity, enthusiasm, valour, and hope. At that utterance when first heard, once more men must have felt "a man-child is born into the world;" and the government shall be upon his shoulders—note especially, the do, do, la, do sharp, passage, and other culminations. Here, though Beethoven has not surpassed, if rivalled, the "Allegro" of Op. 13, he has given it a worthy counterpart. We are invigorated, and cheered—nay, roused to enthusiasm; poured full of virtuous resolve and noble daring. *Lebe hoch der junge Beethoven! Au reste*—we should have to use much colder language for the other movements (except the splendid minuet, so superior to the trio, which also suggests incongruity—unless we like to call it contrast?). The andante seems in no way superior to Haydn, and becomes veritably *langweilig*. How inferior to the "Andante, Op. 26!" The rondo is, comparatively, mere trifling—we are inclined to say, unworthy of Beethoven. We have no real pleasure in playing it, but constantly think, "Oh, for the first movement!" Summing up this symphony, we may perhaps decide : On the whole, guilty of incongruity—of want of proper consciousness. Why this halting between the pastoral and warlike? If your "as a whole" theory is good for a movement, why not for a symphony? due allowance for contrast excepted. Certainly, it may be said, the symphony is of unequal value ; and that had Beethoven given us all equal to the "Allegro," it would have been a truly great symphony, quite worthy of his great name. As it is, the allegro and minuet alone partake of the immortal.

SYMPHONY II.   OPUS 36.

THE ADAGIO.

The worn-out despot offered a premium for a new pleasure ; the critic would often do so for a new epithet. How shall I characterize this exquisite prelude? It is as the portico to the Walhalla of the gods. Here we have the real Beethoven in his *divine* profundity—profound, *because* beautiful; its very beauty constituting the depth, as it were, *thickening* into it, like the ocean and heaven. This beauty, the true Proteus, is evasive; its import was not clear to the utterer himself, no message of the Divine is, to the human vehicle—

"A coral conduit ivory cisterns filling."

We cannot exactly translate or interpret it, only we feel that *were* it translated, we should have a divine poem in a divine language. One could spend hours going into the details of it—for every note demands a word; those two opening ones namely. How characteristic! There is the Emperor Tone-Poet, Napoleon of music, commanding "Attention!" and not— God forbid!—for himself, but for his message. It is the "Thus saith the Lord" of the prophet (some Elijah) of old. Utterance so simple—so all-compelling! Those two notes, merely, are, as it were, like the slightest scratch of an apostle. Then the next three bars! They at once usher us into that ineffability of Beethoven's which we spoke of. We have no reluctance to admitting that originality is not particularly studied here. Nay, we are inclined to say something higher—the modesty and moral courage to reject originality is displayed. Beethoven had to deliver that "Thus saith the Lord!" and he did it. First feel, and then study, the *un*studied eloquence of it. It is one of the beautiful instances whose name is legion in Beethoven, of simplicity—

"In its simplicity sublime."

To me it says—"There! the storms *are* all fought

out. Peace, after all, is at the bottom, and in the heart." Or it is like a high man—say Beethoven himself—after the despicable petty disgusts, as well as chaotic horrors of life, falling back upon nature, the eternal star-glimmering universe—" they will not repel and deceive me, they are everlasting and sublime!" The phrase—like every great message—is really indescribable except by itself; the profound peace, or rather peaceful profundity of it, are unutterable—

"O that my tongue could utter "—

It is a great instance of height towering out of depth, high because deep, a peak in music, yet not clad with eternal glacier, except for its purity of heart, but eternal sunbeams.

After an interesting passage of "harmonious breathing " interposed, and the still more interesting one of chromatic part-repetition, the shakes—which are ultimately to play a great part—first make their appearance. The taste for the shake can soon degenerate; and Beethoven himself sometimes used it incontinently. But, when properly introduced, as here, and especially at the last, it is an ornament that has a more or less magical charm.

The next noble bit reminds us a little of the "Funeral March" in the A flat Sonata. Thereupon Beethoven, in his unconscious or conscious unconscious progress, promulgates some of these characteristic utterances of his—those harmonious and melodic breathings, so profound and pregnant with we know not what. Who or what moved him to his wonderful "progressions?" Truly indescribable tone-poet! so deep with tenderness, so rich with glow—glow is where Beethoven exceeded all of them, especially the Saxon school; he added glow to height, breadth, and

depth ; or, rather, his glow and depth—as in the sun
—are like cause and effect, one.

Now follow those warblings—

"Wild bird ! whose warble liquid sweet
Rings Eden through the budded quicks,"

and "deep answering unto deep," which we mentally
alluded to at the outset, hard to decipher, seraphically
beautiful.   In what a musical river, to employ another
figure, or concourse of confluences, the inspired
orchestra rolls on ; for yes, verily, the river is inspired
with utterance, big with its message. And this
is no merely European river, but rather some tropical
Zambesi or Amazon with its colossal origin and
surroundings ; or, again, the river that rolls from
the throne of the Fountain of Life—which truth it
seems to declare, in the magnificent emphatic passage (anticipating the choral symphony ?) so originally
grand, in D minor, in unison, mark that.   It seems
to say—" Hear that, and believe it.   The rolling
river which this universe is, does not flow from Chaos
and Diabolus, but from Eternal Self-Justified Will—
humanly named, in short, 'God' ; as it were, takes
its course through the bosom of God, as ' King John'
wished the rivers of his realm to, through his."   After
this colossal passage, we seem to be invited to listen
to the warblings and happy murmurs in the halls of
heaven—the habitation of the blest, of just spirits
made perfect.   It is all delicately, crystallinely ineffable ; and the language of imaginative sympathy
itself can scarcely transcend the beauty and exceeding
excellence of the whole movement—that profound
inspiration—any more than it can transcend the beauty
and exceeding excellence, amounting to divinity, of
the universe, that "Midsummer Night's Dream !"

THE ALLEGRO.

I often doubt, war can never cease, for its element is so great and potent in art—especially music and her twin-sister, poetry. Carlyle specially speaks of the "great stroke, too, that was in Shakespeare, had it come to that;" and, indeed, makes this—together with the "so much unexpressed in him to the last "—in short, his infinitude, the very thing which Schubert's kindred eye saw in Beethoven, differentiating him, his two chief points of admiration and test in general of a man. Besides, in our great historian himself—in Milton, too—we feel that there was a great stroke, as of the sublime Ironside ; before him, in Dante ; before him, in Homer—perhaps, Virgil ; but not Horace. In our own day, the noble ring of our poet-laureate's verse, to mention no more, is at once a voucher for the same fact, apart from his "Maud," and more than one indignant utterance. The poetic imagination and classic beauty of all such men is not only concomitant with, but inseparable from, a "good stroke in them" (Dante and Cervantes were actually on the battle-field)—from an heroic element, the best thing they have. The greatest utterance—inspiration—cannot possibly come from any other. The hero is dear to God ; the coward perhaps most despised of all. And why? The reason is philosophical enough. Because the soul of the universe is power—and without courage there can be no goodness. The grand doctrine of evolution, penetrating everywhere, has brought home to us, and borne in upon us, that there is not a field or a grove which is not the theatre of perpetual struggle—not one manifestation exempt from it. *Vae victis* is the word of Nature herself, and the "struggle" is divinely ordained (competition is the salt of existence) for the elaboration of energies—the eventuation in higher life. What man would wish for the *dolce far niente* of the Fool's Paradise ? The world hath been groaning and travailing until now, and must for a long, long time to come ; only one-fourth of it is even now " civilized," and in that civilisation what dregs and dens of barbarism seem ineradicable. All sorts of wrong still tyrannise; therefore, spiritually and physically, the warrior must stand forth great to wage war against the bad everywhere, politically and intellectually—against social evils, and art-darkness—against lies, and for truth—against weakness, and for strength ; for Might *is* Right in the universe—weakness is one with evil, strength with good. Only the good is strong ; only the bad is weak.

We have been led into these remarks by dwelling on the fact, how frequently the warlike spirit manifests itself forth in our Beethoven—indeed, is irrepressible ; nay, I am urged to say, cardinal. In spite of Beethoven's truly divine beauty, he is stamped and distinguished by power. When he issues young into the arena, we see " victorious success" gleaming on his brows. Handel is distinguished in the same way. Hence the secret of Beethoven's own hero-worship for him. Apollo is great, but Jupiter is greater—Jupiter Optimus Maximus. If Mozart, Weber, Schubert may, more or less, figure as the sun-god, they cannot figure as the god of the sun-god. We might almost say, the first notes of Beethoven proclaimed power. He had to go forth and do battle with things. Nor is his own struggle for existence (not mere being, but immortality—a life in immortality here ; that is existence to your Beethoven) in his own life-element, so strong and chaotic, in his own soul-progress, unde-picted, or shadowed forth. With unconscious-consciousness did he do it—on, right on to the end, the bitter end ; on the verge of blindness, insanity—we know not what. Rushing as he did, into the conflict, conscious only of power, Beethoven would have been struck had he seen what, through the long vista of " stilled splendour and gloom," that power boded and implied : he would have been awed, had it been revealed to him what that power represented—little short of the Nineteenth Century itself, with all its Hamlet doubts, and chaotic, yet germ-rich smouldering of transition, whereof more anon.

If the ineffable adagio—prelude of preludes (?), out, as Marx says, the last movement is the finale of finales—shows us the young God-disguised athlete, with the morning light on his brow, making ready to enter only the Olympian Games, the *allegro con brio* shows him to us rushing into battle ! The " heroic symphony" is by no means the first or last symphony heroic—indeed, could not have been written but for the pre-existence and exercise of that full power in the inspired young composer. Here is a grand epic outburst and onrushing worthy of that immortal masterpiece, and essentially one with it. We could almost say, not only the same power, but the same sort of power, is indiscernible in Haydn and Mozart. The style (which is truly the man—that to the man what the bark is to the tree) is so different—the man's dialect, as well as message ; the phraseology altogether. These modulations are not those of Haydn and Mozart ! (beyond praise grand is the *ff* on the dominant of A minor—one of those glorious bursts and surprises of Beethoven's—we expect D minor) ; nor is the masculine fancy (god-like shall we say ? and a Mozart's, goddess-like) theirs ; and the great broad, quasi-Titanic strains and themes. This

movement (Op. 36) is an advance on that of the
symphony No. 1 (Op. 21), if in grade only, not kind.
Here we see the young giant, not yet done growing,
a little riper.   There is no strain in it which we feel
inclined to qualify, which "gives us pause," like the
second motiv in its predecessor; all is homogeneous,
epically great.   But let us descend a little to details.
At bars 1, 2, and 3, we imagine the firm tread of the
warriors, singing (like the Ironsides before Dunbar—
the 68th Psalm, "Let God arise,") on their way to
victory, which they never doubt for a moment, not
only because they are triumphant veterans, but on
account (and more) of their cause.   At bar 4 what a
poetic rush (inrush) of fifes is suggested! then the
great step is heard again ; a great strain joins in; the
chaunt of the warrior basses becomes more and more
ominous ; preliminary thunder is heard, and at last,
with Olympian pæan and war-cry battle is joined ;—
great is the shock, and glorious is the struggle !

The second subject in A is ushered in by those
grand *third-less* chords (long before our modern
writers) :—

the chromatic passage being doubled two octaves
below by the basses.   The new subject, more absolutely melodious, still keeps up the same theme—(for,
apropos, we may also look upon this allegro as some
Homeric or Shakespearian recital of a great victory—
recall the superb opening lines of "Richard the Third,"
the "warriors' wreathed brows, and their bruised arms
hung up for monuments").   At first it is heard softly

—like a reinforcement in the distance (we think of the Prussians at Waterloo, in the westering summer sun)— then as it were in a blaze of music bursts in. Immediately after, where its exquisite first half (so simple—mark that—but so eloquent and picturesque) reappears in the basses (high), we are rather reminded of Mendelssohn's "Huntsman's Song without Words," in A (the same key), Book 1 ; but—we need not say— Mendelssohn has not gilded gold, or improved the lily ; for his fancy was distinctly lighter and smaller than Beethoven's—or, let us say, he had fancy, Beethoven imagination. And now a happy spirit of triumph sings in the basses : and then burst out some crashing Beethoven-chords, of which I will but point to the one *ff* (5th bar of them) ; it is characteristically the 6—4 of D—not, as anticipated, the 5—3 of F♯ minor.

Then, after a foreboding crescendo—characteristic growth out of an initial fragment—and these two emphatic notes :—

—Beethoven all over—the first part closes, so to say, in a breadth of thunder-peals and fiery rain. Technically, note the grand entry of D minor, and mi—do— si—la—mi in unison, with the 3rd omitted ; and the minor-seventh chords, resolving into the tonic dominant of the minor (D[1]), so exquisitely expressive— alike of the pangs of victory and the heroic resolution to endure them.

In the 2nd Part, on the way to G minor (Beethoven himself often never knew whither he was taking us,

or at least the precise route—and so much the better !), we soon meet with a remarkable juncture of
notes, viz., do and mi of the chord (G minor), with fa
superadded :—

This fa, at first sight perplexing, turns out to be a
stray note (as it seems) of the minor seventh chord
on its way to the seventh, which, however, ultimately
appears (with beautiful effect) as the 3rd of the domi-
nant-seventh chord (to C minor). This powerfully,
painfully expressive dissonance is likewise to be found
in his "Lied Vom Tode" (Op. 48), amongst other
instances; and the opening to Schubert's "Wanderer"
owes its intense expression to the same. The *raison
d'être* of such discords is perhaps to be found in the
enhancement they give to the resolution. We could
not bear them too long, or too frequent ; but, as a
passing reminder of the tragedy of life, they profoundly move and interest us ; and, perhaps, discords in
life (likewise instituted by no Dryasdust) have essentially the same *raison d'être* and explanation—life is
agro-dolce, not *dolce* alone, and better so. Thereupon
we have a new idea, surely as playfully felicitous and
characteristic as the scherzo of the " Eroica" itself—
like the warriors at sport. after victory ; or like a
glimpse of the same by them, back in a pause in the
battle, which soon recommences, with the shouts of
the combatants and groans of the wounded and
dying. A page farther on, we have a truly sublime
episode ; great is the chaunt on the earnest theatre
(proclaiming Right must and shall win) made up of the

sufficient chord of F sharp minor, and the basses moving in such a way as served as a model for Wagner; this is epic, heroic, indeed! and—even greater—Pelion upon Ossa, piled by this Titan fighting on the side of the gods, is the culmination. Semitone by semitone mount the basses; and over all the great clouds become richer in the setting sun, and pealing hosts of heaven (as it were) join in the shouts of the victors, crying—"Hosanna in excelsis! Alto trionfo del regno verace! Right *is* done!"

> "Glory of warrior, glory of orator, glory of song,
> Paid with a voice flying by, to be lost on an endless sea.
> Glory of virtue to fight! to struggle, to right the wrong,
> Give her the glory of going on, and still to be."

The Larghetto.

At the moment we write, all round us we see nature emerged—

> "Nobler and balmier for her bath of storm."

The grim tempests of early winter have passed over, and after a South-Italian night—a perfect blaze of constellations, with the Evening Star incredible in the west, large, lustrous, evanescent—and Orion sublime in the forehead of the Night over the mountain—with Jupiter passed over, Mars and Sirius not far off, and the eternal cluster of the Pleiades (those beautiful heralds) winging its flight towards the north-west, and the leading star of the Ursus Major plunging through the dusk (yet shining) over Naples; after such a night, lo! the great amphitheatre of the world is a spectacle indeed! The mountain-island sweeps like a garden at our feet to the sea; the sea itself like an unspeakable floor or carpet spread out *for us*, bearing the islands—the " great globe itself "—so proudly on its nourishing bosom ; and all round, out of a tender dusk (as it were, like Compassion) rises the snow-peaked world (like virtue clothing beauty, reason crowning power), the magnificent spur of the Alps —showing what mountains can do at an effort—called the Apennines, stretching down and around from Gaeta to Alicote, towering over treasures, as it seems, of unearthly beauty ; Monte St. Angelo, with h·s colossal foot in the sea and roots in the world, his wrinkles lined with snow, looms and towers before us ; on the right sweeps and bares itself the grand Bay of Salerno, and on the left the proud Bay of Naples, with its eternal Watch-fire, like a sentinel over all. Stupendous scene of beauty and power! and all that—on this heavenly morning, when the world once more seems made again, and to overpower us with its reiteration of Immortality—all that comes before us as a grand subject set to music in this larghetto of Beethoven's ; all that, too—if the fancy may be allowed—seems in the key of A natural. Before *it*, we should like to hear this exquisite masterpiece-- this, I will not say, Song without Words, but rather Te Deum laudamus—adequately performed, say by the Künstler of his " Vaterland." Here we have a sweetness and a serenity the more touching, because they are *not* those of a Mozart, but a Beethoven ; those of nature, "*nobler and balmier* for her bath of storm" (human as well as physical nature); whether Mozart do or do not represent the storm already fought out, this is the sweetness, not of sweetness. but depth—the serenity, not of serenity, but power. And, indeed, we must hold, and urge, that however the objective may be of value, and rank pre eminent in poetry, the greatest music has come down to us from perhaps the greatest subjective soul; and essentially, much of contemporary, morbidly-conscious music seems in comparison not only objective but material, not only material but sensational; the delusively brilliant (phosphorescently brilliant) product of a decaying time—we had almost said the elaborate effeteness of a written-out age.

This larghetto is of Beethoven's first period, ripened of course (strive as refiners may, they will scarcely be able to alter the time-honoured division, so obviously founded in truth). Haydn and Mozart are distinctly discerned glimmering through it, but not very much more; it is Haydn and Mozart *plus* Beethoven, which makes all the difference. We repeat, it is *his* serenity and sweetness, his youth (so full and rich—of such *infinite* promise), not theirs. Theirs be the grace, but his the grandeur; theirs the amiability, but his the milk of human kindness—so broad and deep (as of a yet unsoured Hamlet, an Othello, a King Lear : for there are great characters in Shakespeare which we *can* blend Beethoven with, but not the others). The details of the larghetto must be studied (say, at the organ). I will here only advert to its reminiscence of the andante (the exquisite episode) in the pastoral sonata, written about the same period, truly worthy of symphonic treatment, with the deliciously-delicate passage, as it were like a shower of sunbeams, of gold sparkles—

" In the æther of Deity "

as the manifestations named men have been called). The movement is rich both in the great strokes and tender touches of genius—of genius which is power ; and what we call the phraseology of the man as a whole, and in its parts, is again beautifully Beetho venian.   Here is a lovely bit:—

The movement is not so *great* as the preceding, and is perhaps too long (which is a decided art-fault—not merely a mistake in judgment) ; but, as a whole, it reminds us of Shakespeare's "entire and perfect chrysolite ;" we greet it (and other movements of Beethoven's) with feelings of profound affection ; as though we had realised those words "Yet a little while and ye have me with ye "; as though we had been living, for at least a breathing space, in the atmosphere and society of higher life, out of the sphere of time and in the sphere of the eternal.   We have had such pleasure that we feel more good ; we issue grateful and earnest, happier, better men. There have been sighs of regret that Beethoven did not write more music like his Symphony in F ; but not only this movement, but these two first sym phonies, the sonatas in E flat, "Adelaide"—nay, almost all his first period compositions.   And here our glances at this symphony must cease.   The trio, with its delicious strain, pleases us more than the scherzo (a strain that might be made much more of). The scherzo itself is less sympathetic than that of No. 1 : seems, in fact, rather heavily frolicsome.   The finale is a masterpiece, though decidedly inferior to the first movements. Do composers often write their finale when they are jaded? they should make this their golden rule, *toutes les choses ont leur matinée.*

SYMPHONY No. III., OP. 55.

"Lo Motor primo a lui si volge licto,
Soora tant'arte di natura, e spira
Spirito nuovo, di virtù repleto"—

When we stand before this Symphony, like Death, it "gives us pause"; it looms so great, so vast. It was no wonder that it was not comprehended at first; and this should be not a subject of regret, but gratification, to the genius. Genius implies non-comprehension at first, and all sorts of "cold obstruction"; and here it may at once be said that, on the whole, genius, like virtue, is its own reward, and perfect compensation for all drawbacks. This should be borne in mind when uncalled-for lamentations are, not unnaturally, yet rather thoughtlessly made. Certainly, Beethoven would not have been satisfied had this phenomenal work, this prodigy, this spiritual Labour of Hercules (type of all the great Helpers and Saviours of mankind), been immediately grasped. To comprehend, in some small measure, the prodigy called the Universe around us, men and things have had to evolve for countless ages; it is the same, on a miniature scale, with individual works; and every poet rids himself of his message in the great spirit of the great Kepler:—
"I may well wait a century for a reader, as God has waited six thousand years for an observer." To no man not rich in such a spirit will any great message be whispered and entrusted.

Beethoven was, in his sphere, and with his vehicle

of utterance, a prophet—a coming event that threw its shadow before.   He revealed to men, if they could but have seen it, the Nineteenth Century—*its* inner life, *plus* the nature and passions of the present (his own day) and the past.   No wonder, then, that the men of his own day—the great mass, the local majority—could not understand what really is a truer mirror of us—our doubts, and fears, and struggles, and hopes.   And the *Sinfonia Eroica*, I take it, must be so interpreted—in a spiritual sense (at least as well as in the physical, or literal)—as much as the Symphony in C minor, at least as much as the Pastoral Symphony which Beethoven himself said was really emotional rather than descriptive.   And it little matters whether or not Beethoven himself consciously uttered these manifold messages of his in this or that sense ; he has as perfect a right as Shakespeare to be deemed full of all that can be packed into him ; nay, it is all the better if he was *not* conscious : to repeat —unconsciousness was the soul of his consciousness, as it ever is, and must be, of all higher speech and performance.

No mere battle, or ordinary warfare—certainly Napoleonic—can adequately explain, is solely depicted in, this grand work ; though they become far more satisfactory, so applied, when we consider them as coarse manifestations of the higher qualities ; in fact, as backgrounds for and revelations of heroism. By dwelling on this, we get nearer to the soul of the symphony ; spiritual warfare, rather, is what it proclaims.*   Of Beethoven's notes, it may be quite as

---

* Strauss (*not* the dance composer), in rather a cavilling spirit, says this symphony describes the life of a hero.   So it does, but not in the external sense he uses it in, but in the internal ; life, means inner life.   Or, again, the work celebrates heroism rather than a hero.

much said as of Luther's words—·his notes are like other men's battles. Better than any poem this symphony (especially the first movement—*facile princeps*) seems to hold the mirror up to Man in his Warfare, specially and generally, physically and spiritually, with and in his own inscrutable self, and with and in the unspeakable elements of time. It is not without special beauty, in the last but one, or Faust sense (we were struck and pleased to come across Bendel's words, corroborating our own notion, that Beethoven was in some sort a Faust); and, before this symphony, we feel Beethoven was that good man, struggling with adversity, the spectacle of which is a benefit to the very gods; and, under this feeling, the symphony does us double good. The fact on the face of it is, its Titanic power in *maturity*. The first two symphonies, also rich in power, are stamped by a spirit of youth. This gives them a delicious charm which makes them extra dear; and which Beethoven himself (let alone others) was fundamentally mistaken (we feel) in underrating, nay, disparaging, as he was afterwards wont to do (really, when his mighty powers were waning, and he was perhaps in secret aware of that; it is the common melancholy trick of men). That peculiar spirit of freshness here at length we seem to miss, or are no longer struck by. Here we may draw the line. Here we see the ripe man, or very nearly so; at least in the prime and plenitude of his powers; not quite so *happy* as before, but stronger; and as yet with no serious threatening shadow of gloom—though there may be clouds "as big as a man's hand," and even occasionally, perhaps, hints, like the mole "cinque-spotted i' the bottom of a cowslip," of tragedy and aberration among the most melancholy in the history of men.

Beethoven was an emphatically conscious, but profoundly unconceited man. We are sure, therefore, that he entitled his symphony "Heroic" (if he did do so) with no unpardonable vanity; nevertheless, we regret that (as also in his "Grand" sonatas) he did not leave it to others—for itself to call itself that. Truly, he did not exceed much in betitling and programming—his sense of the infinitude of music was too profound, of that as being *the* charm; but even in the few cases where he did, perhaps the breach would have been better than the observance. One great disadvantage of betitling music is, that it does not allow us to approach it afterwards without preoccupation and convention; whereas, we should approach it utterly free, except from our own nature, and previous existence. Moreover, if the work correspond ever so to the title or description, it is discounted beforehand. To say *afterwards*, "that is heroic!"—"this is pastoral!" is an added charm. But to details.

It will at once be noticed that Beethoven begins this symphony quite differently from its predecessors; *allegro con brio*, two emphatic chords, and then *in medias res;* the bass, however, leading off, as in No. II., with, moreover, the same well-balanced poise (delicate, yet firm as that of planet in its orbit), springy step, and self-contained power. A characteristic originality is the C sharp, where the bass breaks off, hardly begun, and the

"Upper air bursts into life,"

with glorious breadth and soaring— soaring to the *primum mobile* through obstructive cloud (discords of the dim. 7th on pedal tonic) with only increased *éclat!* Thereupon, the basses worthily how forth the heroic confidence of the nobly unstudied theme —great and gay with the certainty of final victory; as it were, the warriors of Israel advancing to conquer the Promised Land. Then, from none knows where —from the very heart of heaven—fall shafts of light indeed, as it were through the bosom of fragrance; which exquisite strain, perhaps, contradicts what we said about the absence of youth in this work. In any case, it is one of those many melodies which so movingly proclaim Beethoven a profoundly good man, and how he wrote them so *from above*, or rather they poured through him from infinite heights (depths overhead) of ineffability. In this, in the *power* of his sweetness, he has never been surpassed, hardly equalled.

There are melodies by later men very beautiful too, which seem, however, to come (we are almost tempted to write) like certain later poetry, from a profoundly *bad* source; they have demoniac, not divine beauty. The strain in question :—

Certainly a

"Dolce melodia in aria luminosa,"

seems the spirit of Love itself pure and simple—as it were, a glance from the "young-eyed cherubim" into the Warrior's—into Beethoven's own heart. But, in this "painfully earnest world," such blessedness cannot long last, and the sunshafts are soon again obscured in the smoke of battle—the mystic whisperings drowned in the din of artillery. *Apropos,* it struck us that, if we like the warlike figure, this grand battlepiece (by Rubens? or Tintonello?—*Rembrandt*, we would rather say) gains, if we consider it as a *sea*-battle, in a storm, with wizard lights and seams of fire all along the horizon. Nay, in the second part—those wonderful strokes of genius where the chord of the sub dominant (?) is piled on to and clashes against that of the relative minor A— we fancy it vividly depicting "Nelson falls!" (the true hero, whose pole-star is duty; not pleasure, nor ambition); and the unspeakable passage a little further on (in E minor—Beethoven alone capable of it—never dreamt of in the philosophy of his predecessors), suggested his death—(or rather, more stupendously, that of *the* Christian Hero, when He "gave up the ghost," crying, "*Finitus est!*").

More than one modern work has attempted to depict the world-old great subject: Virtue and Vice contending for (or within) a human soul—the struggle of Good and Evil. Methinks, as long ago as this Heroic Symphony the same struggle is represented, or shadowed forth (for its great text, like music in general, and more so with Beethoven, has many meanings). The third (?) subject in this theme-rich movement, where Beethoven from his full heart pours forth one motiv after another, is especially suggestive of conflict—what shocks, clashes, contentions!—but the "good angel fires the bad one out," and bears the precious prize aloft in a whirl of triumph—resounding, as it were, through the halls of heaven—

> "Whose Titan angels, Gabriel, Abdiel,
> Starr'd from Jehovah's gorgeous armouries,
> Tower, as the deep-domed empyrean
> Rings to the roar of an angel onset."

But then—

> "Me rather all that bowery loveliness,
> The brooks of Eden mazily murmuring,
>   And bloom profuse and cedar arches
>   Charm, as a wanderer out in ocean,"

> "Where some refulgent sunset of India
> Streams o'er a rich ambrosial ocean isle,
>   And, crimson-hued, the stately palm-woods
>   Whisper, in odorous heights, of even."

Then we have a strain which seems to anticipate Schumann himself, the greatest symphonist after Beethoven—a singular repose, of almost unearthly loveliness, after the high commotion.

A little later, and *ecco !* a new idea :—

exquisite in its lightness and strength (like a giant at play, or a river disporting in its banks) ; and thereupon, after bold progressions, six remarkable iterations—also like "So Fate knocketh at the portals !" or like blow after blow of virtuous resolutions ; where all is characteristic, this is strikingly so. Then follows another of his ineffable thoughts (supremely) ; and then, after another whirl of the *sacred* fury, which seems to be the soul of this unexampled movement, we are brought back to the original subject, which re-enters in its own colossal continence ; and these truly "*stupendi pagine*" (and not those about Goethe's Frederika of Sessenheim, in his " Autobiography,") are repeated. The second part, or elaboration (as it is called, is likewise, and *par excellence*, stupendous, especially the part before adverted to, in A and E minor.   Here, truly, the music quite transcends ordinary language and thought; to bring ideas worthy to it, we must recur to Him who cried "*Lama, Lama, Eli Sabbacthani!*"   This is the anguish of a Redeemer-soul.   But to such, also, is the victory; and to such the Father sendeth legions of angels.   See, also, especially the passage further on, in G flat (should it not be *andante?*)—which, as it were, almost overcomes us with enchantment.   Here, methinks, the Invisible Auxiliaries already bear the poor shell, and whisper at the same time a word of comfort to the Mother—whom no Power strikes into stone, like Niobe.

"He that hath ears to hear, let him hear!"—ears that are but the outwork of the soul.   Let him go, even as it were, prepared and attuned, in some sort like a Communicant—and receive music's banquet mysteriously provided for him.   The message of a Beethoven is not trifling, but earnest; speaks inarticulately (more divinely so) of the greatest, solemnest, things; whispers and thunders from the Altar.   If "the value of no word is known till the greatest master of it has arrived," so also the value of no utterance is known till the greatest receiver—understander—of it has arrived.   Plato said, Poets speak greater things than they know.   Of none was this ever truer than of Beethoven.   He alone, in his day, most knew the value and import of his music; others come after (and will come) who know more.   This is his greatest praise.   There is no more congenial occupation to a sympathetic imagination than throwing together some of the images, thoughts, or ideas which his mighty music suggests.   Goethe was displeased when importuned for the key-idea (*more Ger-*

manico) of his "Wilhelm Meister;" thought that itself should be sufficient of itself. It is the same with Beethoven and this symphony. No *rigid* principle must be sought, or insisted on. The first movement especially does indeed stand very four-square and homogeneous; but the fiery soul of it (sun-fire, passion and beauty,) is very various in its manifestation; and unless we understand and apply the term "heroic" in its amplest sense, we are fettered and injured rather than benefitted and helped. The greatest Hero we yet wot of was personified self-sacrifice, love—who did not flame abroad over that world a devastation, but made his life answer the queries of philosophy, and the doubts of the sceptic; the greatest Hero was one who "went about doing good."

Tennyson's eloquent alcaics on Milton—

> "O mighty-mouth'd inventor of harmonies,
> O skill'd to sing of Time or Eternity"—

the rest of which have been already quoted, seems not inapplicable to Beethoven and this his symphony. Many others would do as well, or better. Of general application—when we *think* of its melodious rush of ideas (one of the distinguishing features between it and the first two symphonies), great republican spirit (in the highest sense), Sun-god beauty, and Jove-like power; of its intellect, superior to that of Bach's (it seems to us), as Carlyle well says Shakespeare's was to that of the author of "*Novum Organum*," and of its grace and sweetness, profounder than, not only of Haydn's and Mozart's, but any other composer's, then the beautiful words of Dante, at the head of this chapter, may apply.

The Prime Mover turns joyfully unto him, and, surpassing nature, breathes into him a new spirit, replete with virtue and power.

THE FUNERAL MARCH.

Beethoven was a gloomily profound soul ;—herein differentiated from Shakespeare, who was pellucidly, cheerfully profound; and unlike Schopenhauer (whom he otherwise rather suggests), who was profoundly gloomy—one of the most so who ever lived ; therefore he composed a "*Marcia Funèbre*" specially *con amore*, and therefore it is specially characteristic of him. In the present instance, this, as it were, unfathomably profound inspiration, gains, as in every other case, if we interpret it liberally rather than literally, and consider it to depict and deplore rather the death of a great Principle (such as Faith, Virtue, Truth,) than a great man ; or the great man, the hero, *plus* the heroic, buried with him, *ultimus Romanorum* If we would realize the depths of this utterance— as it were almost speechless—choked with tears— we shall think of it in connection with such words as the following :—

> "Tired with all these, for restful death I cry—
> As to behold desert a beggar born,
> And needy nothing trimm'd in jollity,
> And purest faith unhappily forsworn,
> And gilded honour shamefully misplaced,
> And maiden virtue rudely strumpeted,
> And right perfection wrongfully disgraced,
> And strength by limping sway disabled,
> And art made tongue-tied by authority,
> And folly (doctor-like) controlling skill,
> And simple truth miscall'd simplicity,
> And captive good attending captain ill ;
> Tired with all these, from these I would be gone,
> Save that, to die, I leave my love alone."

Speaking of Schopenhauer, the difference between him and Beethoven seems to be this :—the latter shows us Optimism *victorious* over Pessimism ; his works, indeed, seem specially and wonderfully to mirror the struggle, as indeed, the whole of this century at least is profoundly tinctured, nay seems almost characteristically stamped by Pessimism ; but Beethoven does not, and will not give way to, and end in the rayless paralysis of Pessimism ; he fights through, and soars triumphant ; in Mr. Picton's words, *re* Materialism, " comes out at the other side." In this, methinks, the deadly struggle betwixt Optimism and Pessimism around us and within us ; but the victory of the former, and the triumph of Immortality over Doubt and Denial, we have the key to Beethoven's music (of course unconsciously, and, as we say, so much the better ; it would have been worse expressed had it been conscious). At a moment when Pessimism was uppermost, he might have sat down to write this Dead March : that it was to celebrate Napoleon Buonaparte was never the case, though it might have been to celebrate the Napoleon of Beethoven's imagination, a *Hero,* to bewail whose departure from among us no tones can be too pregnant and profound, especially if we think we have "fallen on evil times," and that we shall "never look upon his like again." And here a word about Beethoven's (the true hero) immortal act, when he heard that Napoleon had made himself crowned—(the other hero we spoke of refused a crown, and hid himself) ; was not *that* a repudiation of Tyranny and Quackery? was not *that* a royal piece of Iconoclasm? to me it is one of the highest private scenes of History. Summon it up one moment :—Beethoven's eye flashing fire ; the lion locks almost shaking flames, as he tears the superscription in half (and Napoleon's fame with it), and dashes the " carefully written out " symphony on the floor, " put his foot down on *that.*"

So, I should like to see Beethoven painted ; or still
better, sculptured.   Dr. Nohl has taken occassion to
draw an elaborate parallel or comparison between
Beethoven and another great contemporary of his,
Goethe—(we would draw it also to the advantage of
the former ; Carlyle has done so, between Napoleon
and Goethe ; we would. do so between Napoleon and
Beethoven, and call the latter in our great Sage's
words, a "still white light shining far into the centuries," while the other was meteoric flame and vol-
canic glare—not wholly, solely, for he too was an
instrument—an able, and necessary one, but in comparison.   Let anyone ask himself how he feels at the
mention of the two names.   Is he not expanded,
cheered, comforted, and made better—unconsciously
made surer of goodness, truth, immortality, and all
high things, at the name of Beethoven ; and is he
not repelled, if dazzled, by that of Napoleon ?   The
good was not buried with Beethoven's bones.   Think
of the amount he has done after his death (like
Handel and his " Messiah ") ; think of his indus-
trious great life and character—so originally grand ;
and contrast it with the portentous mass of lies and
murders, the conflagrations and widow's tears, the
hideous battle-fields of the heartless, semi-conscious,
semi-quack, diabolically selfish Napoleon, and the
good *he* has done after him.   No ! the good Wolfe
had rather have been Gray than the victor of Quebec,
and we would rather have been Beethoven than
Napoleon—whose very genius, moreover, is over-
rated ; for we decidedly think with Madame de Stäel,
that had he met with an able and honest adversary
early, he would have been checked or defeated ; nay,
he *was*, when he met Sydney Smith at Acre ; and,
curiously enough, after, when he met *another* Briton,

who was never defeated—Wellington. Napoleon
will always be marvelled at and written about, but it
will never be said of him—"in his works you will find
enrichers of the fancy, strengtheners of virtue, a
withdrawing from all selfish and mercenary thoughts,
a lesson of all sweet and honourable thoughts and
actions, to teach them courtesy, benignity, generosity,
humanity; for, of examples teaching these virtues,
his pages are full;"—as it was said of the author of
" Hamlet," and as it is here repeated of the mighty
composer of this ' Dead March," with its wails from
the deepest and strains from the highest thing known
—the heart of man.

THE SCHERZO.

With a glance at the Scherzo, we will bring our
remarks to a close, the more especially as the Finale
seems less interesting, relevant, and original (Beethoven seems more to have copied himself,) than the
rest.

The Scherzo, with its *obbligato* constituent element,
the " Trio," is on the same great scale, and in the
same epic spirit (we see no particular need, with
Wagner, to seek a connection,) as the first movement. Here we *see* the gods and heroes, the immor-
tals, at sport in their own high hall—green-hill'd
theatre, and " deep-domed empyrean." Here Optimism is not only victor, but full of play and humour.
Such Olympian sport, such great picturesque music,
was inconceivable to Beethoven's predecessors; and
we get some idea of his merit when we reflect that
the ground, when he began to write quartets and
symphonies, seemed already occupied, the sphere

exhausted ; and when we reflect, how, of all Haydn's
119 symphonies (!) not one, in some seasons, is
performed ; whereas, Beethoven's are the feature of
almost every performance, and are found now to be
"favourite with all classes," as the Sydenham programme asserts—a statement which, otherwise, rather
provokes an elevation of the eyebrows.   The trio,
especially, is of exceeding original beauty ; there are
few more grateful pages in Beethoven ; none where
his peculiarly characteristic *healthy* sweetness (fresh-
ness-and-power—*depths* of purity, beyond plummet's
sound,) is so strikingly, so enchantingly displayed.
At the base of a great mountain in Switzerland, with
his foot in two lakes, and with sides that might
almost have been an envy in Eden, there runs—from
one magical sheet of water to the other—a heavenly
valley.   There we once saw a local military *Fest,*
with flying banners and echoing music ; and, as we
walked along, under the eternal brow of that immense
emerald bastion, with the spring sun before us, we
thought of this Trio, and said.—"Here is where it
ought to sound, by a noble army on its return, laurel-
laden, from righteous victory ;" and Shakespeare's
lines again *festeggiavano* in the memory :—

> "Now is the winter of our discontent
> Made glorious summer by this sun of York ;
> And all the clouds that lower'd upon our house
> In the deep bosom of the ocean buried.
> Now are our brows bound with victorious wreaths ;
> Our bruisèd arms hung up for monuments ;
> Our stern alarums chang'd to merry meetings ;
> Our dreadful marches to delightful measures.
> Grim-visag'd war hath smooth'd his wrinkled front ;
> And now, instead of mounting barbèd steeds,
> To fright the souls of fearful adversaries,
> He capers nimbly in a lady's chamber,
> To the lascivious pleasing of a lute."

How exquisitely we can fancy the horns making those mountain-walls and woodlands ring! and the hautboys in response, gladdening the pastures; while the flutes (later) curl the wave; and the bassoons, along with the other two epico-pastoral instruments, after the maiden welcome of the violins—welcome by maidens :—

"Oneste e leggiadre in ogni atto."—

"Set all the bells a-ringing—over lake and lea,
Merrily, merrily, along with them in tune."

It is all enchanting; no greater epico-lyric poem in Beethoven—who, even in the midst of this triumph and beauty, cannot (thank inspiration!) but speak from the profundities of him. I allude to that wonderful passage where he brings in (hitherto reserved) the clarinets (that voice of heroic women, as Berlioz finds it), over the intensely expressive progression of the strings, in response to the breathings of the horns. In music perhaps there is no profounder interchange of heart and soul, of sorrow and affection, touching reminiscence from the lowest well-spring. This, perhaps, is a glance at the "happy autumn days that are no more;" or an heroic wail over the dead and desolated; a glance back at the horrors of war—a thought for the widows and orphans' tears falling even now around; and yet, under all, a stern determination to brook no tyranny, love of duty, and a high submission, cost what it might, to the Supreme Will.

SYMPHONY IN B FLAT, No. 4, OP. 60.

This Symphony is only another proof of Beethoven's kinship with Shakespeare. The terrible romance of "Romeo and Juliet" (where the atmosphere seems loaded with love and doom); the classic grandeur of "Coriolanus" and "Julius Cæsar"; the passionate intensity of "Othello"; the fearful sublimity (depth, as well as height and breadth) of "Macbeth" and "Lear;" the beautiful greatness of the "Tempest"; and the subtlety (seraphic, not demoniac),· tragic picturesqueness, inner life, and almost superhuman power and insight of "Hamlet," are all, more or less (and, indeed, more rather than less), to be found reproduced in Beethoven; and truly, as it is borne in on us, in him, the tone-poet, more than in speech-poet, certainly more than in Schiller and Goethe; more also than in our own men, of whom none after Shakespeare can compare with Beethoven except Milton—and him we reckon inferior. There are indeed two elements of Shakespeare which Beethoven lacks, his characteristic serenity and humour; besides that, *Beethoven's tragedy is the tragedy of his own soul, whereas Shakespeare wrote outside himself.* Beethoven was a colossally subjective storm-tossed spirit (though also eminently objective—none surpasses him in broad vivid painting of images, as well as "the life of the soul";)—the dove of whose ark (to speak figuratively) never found soil for her foot after youth had died out, and the flood fairly set in. But, in his prime, also in the "April of his prime", and at his best, he bears a greater family likeness to the great ancestor than any other man, though he really resembles no one but himself, just like Shakespeare, as we feel after long but futile efforts to pair him with somebody—a fact highly curious and interesting! The kinship, however, is equally striking and fascinating; and nowhere, perhaps, is it more fascinating than in this B flat Symphony, which we are inclined to term *par excellence* beautiful; as its predecessors are powerful and great. Indeed there seems some-thing of the opaline varnish—or rather, lustre, like a leaf's—*from within*—of Mozart; specially beautiful, as *he* is specially beautiful, and is not powerful or great, profound and earnest, grand. But, again, *plus* the grace, there is also, below, the characteristic depth; after all, and as ever, power is *doch* the soul of the beauty—as—and here is our point—in the "Tempest" (and "Midsummer Night's Dream), as in Shakespeare, rather than in Mozart; indeed, we know not but what Haydn's beauty has more a soul of power.

The enchanting spirit of Shakespeare's fairy plays, and the enchanting spirit world, seems that too of this symphony. Here are Puck and Blossom, Oberon and Titania; here are Ferdinand and Miranda—above all, Ariel and Prospero. Prospero, whose sublime spirit shines and rules in this inaugural adagio—adumbration of Chopin (?) which dwarfs Chopin indeed !—is much nearer akin to Schumann. It is like an inspired dream (a Jacob's, or Elijah's, or Daniel's). It seems a great foreshadowing of his later style; in its vagueness it is vast—as it were, a vestibule or forecourt of the Infinite, of higher life; of that beyond, methinks, whereinto Prospero (our own great dear, sad Beethoven, tired of all, and of himself,) sinks his dreamy glance, when he casts away for ever his magic wand (magic only in a lower sphere, where life and character are inferior); "deeper than did plummet sound," and cries, wrapt from the bystanders :—

> " The cloud-capp'd towers, the gorgeous palaces,
> The solemn temples, the great globe itself,
> Yea, all which it inherit, shall dissolve;
> And, like this insubstantial pageant faded,
> Leave not a wrack behind."

In the allegro we seem to continue our analogy—in the wondrous isle itself (Isle of Formosa), "full of strange sights and sounds." Here, not Greek Naiads and Dryads, but Christian sprites and fairy-things, or both in loving rivalry, flit and trip invisibly and visibly; here is freshness! here are sunbeams! here simplicity and sweetness (woodland and pastoral beauty)! And if, in the matchless adagio the sea murmurs round the "still-vext Bermoothes," and Ariel fetches thence dew; here we have all-compelling Prospero commanding the most exquisite airy sport— but not for himself—but for the lovers.

The scherzo (to take that next), forces upon us once more the question—how far did Beethoven, in composing, draw upon his early treasures? This delicious burst—or gush—of inspiration, as it were a moment flashing over, might have been written in the same spring months as that other delicious morsel —specially cherished by us; the scherzo ("Allegro") in E flat, in the early sonata of the same key—which has always seemed to us the very breath of spring itself—a page of nature in April. And why should a Beethoven disparage his early works? were they. not *doch* the works of a Beethoven! Alas, he can never be young again, never after equal them, for their breath and spirit, for the April of their prime.

We should like to hear Liszt or Rubinstein play this morsel arranged. It is as delicate as Heller (whom it indeed anticipates) and Mendelssohn, and strong as Wagner;—but nay, Beethoven will compare only with himself. It is originally exquisite and exquisitely original. It has, too, the same magical, nay, mystical beauty whose glamour is over all this musical mirror of the "Tempest." The imaginative Sonata in D minor, which Beethoven himself referred to the

enchanting drama—especially the first movement—
reflects, I take it, the deeper bases and significance
of the poem ; tempest-tossed man, with his cries to
the Unknowable, almost like a wounded animal, and
rays of sunshine pouring still through storm ; man,
at war with the elements and himself, the elements
without and within him ; man, so lit le on this stu·
pendous stage ; man, so great with his alone-percep·
tion of it ; man, so mean and hateful in his baser
parts, so colossal, so divine in his higher ; so low as
animal (lower than they), so high as hero and sage.
Indeed, the tremendous conflict of outer and inner
life, this appalling discrepancy we seem to meet with
everywhere ; man's struggle with nature, and the
struggle of both with themselves, seems to be the
inner picture both of Shakespeare and Beethoven—
especially the latter, who was a mighty brooding fer-
menting soul—how far transcending our Byron and
his " Manfreds"!—more allied to " Faust," yet
greater, nobler, dearer, difficult to arrive at harmony
with others and himself (" perplext in faith, yet pure
in deeds"), who seems happy only in the first part of
his progress (expedition, undertaking, crusade), and
victorious in the middle ; and whom, alas ! we fancy
almost as despairing of solving the problem (*è pure
troppo per me*) in the end, and going down in the
tempest—yet, like the traditional Vengeur, with guns
all shooting, and flag at the mast-head flying, and
glorified in the setting sun.

I will not dwell on the finale, but conclude with
some fancies suggested by the rarely beautiful adagio
—like a lovely bird from another world, like the
phœnix new born. Here is what Elterlein says of
the finale :—" The truly phantastic, airy, sprite-like
(*elfenartige*), at times even boding twilight" (the

Scotch uncanny gloaming would more approach the original, *Unheimlicht Düstere*—Scotch, by the way, would often marvellously translate German—they have a mass of expressive words which we have not) —"boding twilight, nay, wild culminates, however, only in the fourth movement. How light and vanishing do these tone-pictures hover and pass, what characteristic glooming (*Helldenkel*, clear-gloom) does not envelope this scene too."

Of course, this symphony cannot compare one moment with the Eroica and C minor, for grandeur, opulence, and power; but it is a lovely interlude, giving us a divine moment of gratification and repose —an Italian spring day by a lake, to a tropical one, with its Himalayas and interwoven forest, "like a cathedral with service on the blazing roof."

And now for the adagio! which I will only preface by this admonition, always to be recollected; viz., that whatever fancies or figures music may suggest, and however the abstract terms—such as sweet, tender, vigorous, grand, &c.—may, and must be applied in common to all composers, yet each composer has a special individuality; and *the music that suggests the figures and fancies, the ideas, has, apart from this, for ever a special charm of its own*, which cannot be lost, nor yet transcribed. To those who do not, and to those who do approve the fancies, this charm *per se* remains.

THE ADAGIO.

A work of supererogation, the adagio is still sometimes executed at concerts, which rejoices in the sensational title of "Le trille du Diable;" founded, it is said, on a dream of the composer's (Tartini);

this, simply-named "Adagio," of Beethoven's, then—
in considering which, I mean to surrender myself
wholly to poetry—might be a reminiscence of his
of music, in a dream, by the angel, Gabriel ; or such,
for instance, as might have escorted the seraph when
he descended, and said, "*Ave Maria!*"—or it might
be an unconscious reminiscence of previous existence
of the great and good man ; or the strain the Shepherds heard, in the field, watching their flocks by
night—again, and more specially, a

" Dolce melodia in aria lumino · ,'

through the purple air, mingled with ambrosia, and
the beams of *that* evening star.   Nay, it might have
lulled that head which had nowhere to rest, when
perchance it *did* find some rocky corner ; or Saul of
Tarsus, or Jonah below on the raging sea.   It puts us
in mind of the immortal line—

" After life's fitful fever, he sleeps well."

Ah ! we see therein the great weary spirit of its own
eternal messenger, for once at least, rocked on its waves
and soothed by its balm, in the sea of immortality.   It
is a pleasure to throw together all the ideas with which
it inspires us.   It seems a foretaste of Schumann and
Ernst (" Elegy ") ; it has their glimmering romance,
and Beethoven's own peculiar profound sweetness,
not tainted (at least here and yet) by anything morbid,
or the suspicion of it.   It, too, suggests earlier years
—"*Ach!*" a reminiscence of childhood in Rhine-
land.   It is glamorous, but with the glamour of
Ariel—a spirit of good—the spirit of Shakespeare.

It is tender and beautiful as Jean Paul; deep, sweet,
unutterably.   Methinks it paints this :—

> "Oh sea ! that lately raged and roared—
> Art now unruffled by a breath ?—
> So shall it be, thou Mighty Teacher,
> With us—after Death."

And this :—

> "And balmy drops in summer dark
> Slide from the bosom of the stars."

And this :—

> "When summer's hourly mellowing change
> May breathe with many roses sweet,
> Upon the thousand waves of wheat
> That ripple round the lovely grange."

And this—with peculiar propriety :—

> "Fair ship, that from the Italian shore
> Sailest the placid ocean-plains
> With my lost Arthur's loved remains,
> Spread thy full wings and waft him o'er.
>
> So draw him home to those that mourn
> In vain ; a favourable speed
> Ruffle thy mirror'd mast, and lead
> Through prosperous floods his holy urn.
>
> All night no ruder air perplex
> Thy sliding keel till Phosphor, bright
> As our pure love, through early light
> Shall glimmer on thy dewy decks.
>
> Sphere all your lights around, above,
> Sleep, gentle heavens, before the prow ;
> Sleep, gentle winds, as he sleeps now,
> My friend, the brother of my love."

(Note especially the truly seraphic ineffability of the
passage in G flat).   It is such music as might have
accompanied Him who made the storm his mere
mantle, and the raging sea the mere pathway of

power; of Him who had the right of all men to say —out of whose mouth the word sounded fullest— Peace!

SYMPHONY IN C MINOR, No. 5, OP. 67.

BEETHOVEN might well write an Heroic Symphony, for the very soul of his symphonies is heroism. He *named* one "heroic," but he *wrote* many, including the sonatas, which are unfortunately limited to the piano, whose powers they utterly transcend. Heroism is the soul, and antagonism the substance, through which heroism ultimately fights its way. Beethoven is the Hercules of music (Hercules was in some sort also the Pagan Christ), undertaking labours for men's emancipation and help; beating Hydros down; conquering all sorts of opposition—unconquerable except by love; and, like the antique hero, alas! with an end as tragic. Such comparisons we are obliged to have recourse to, to explain Beethoven's music—its might and significance. "What, then, does this eternal conflict, and victorious heroism storming through, mean?" Ah! how they still paint the conflict of rule and anarchy, of the intellect and reason, of passion and prejudice!

Man is called the microcosm of nature, and music is the microcosm of man; *his* antagonism and heroism, internal as well as external, are herein mirrored. Music is the highest art, because the most spiritual, infinite, self-existent (creating, not copying), and comprehensive. No statue, picture, or pile, can compare with the power of a symphony —which, indeed, all but rivals that of nature herself, of the great world and starry heavens; the secret of

whose power is also the Infinite, with its whispered
promise—its soul—Immortality.   Art is the shadow-
ing forth of the infinite : music does this most, and
Beethoven's is most music.   Music, as we said, is the
microcosm of man.   As the world is comprised in
him—alone realized *by* him, and therefore in some
sort alone existent *in* him, so are his nature and
history comprised in music—his depths and heights,
beauties and deformities, aspirations and passions,
circumstances and powers.   It is the " might, majesty, and dominion," inarticulateness, *profound*
beauty—as it were searching flower-cups with star-
beams : the effluence of a soul deep as heaven
beyond the other side of earth)—of man (not *"etwas,"*
of a man) that Beethoven shadows forth.   That one,
also, who struggled in the womb—what was he but a
type of man in the all-comprising womb of nature ?
And this, also, Beethoven's music suggests ; not least
the music of this stupendous symphony—only another
" Eroica," and greater, without the name (better so).
More suo, Beethoven himself flashed a meaning more
or less on it.   "So knocketh Fate at the portal ;"
yes ! with the portentousness of the " knocking at
the gate" (see Lamb's remarks), in " Macbeth ;"
yes ! fate in the form of duty.   And truly, what
higher subject—subject dear to the ancients as they
are called—subject constantly treated in his own
inspired way (Nature's), by Shakespeare—could be
chosen ?   And Beethoven has rivalled Aiskulos and
Shakespeare.   Here is battle ! here is victory !—here,
too, the air seems almost oppressive with love and
doom ; and here, too, in the background, and from
the deepest deeps, are wreaths and similes of celestial
beauty.   " Well done, good and faithful servant ;
enter thou into the joy of thy Lord."   Another thing

the first movement suggests is, that it is the greatest of "*Dies Iræ.*" That passage, especially on the second page of the second part, where one half the orchestra answers the other with the same terrific unisons—

(*en passant*, did ever reiteration play such a part?), prompts the wildest fancies. We think of

> " The glooms of hell
> Echoed with thunder, while the angels wailed ;"

or again, echoes of deserted hell on the day of doom —the fiends summoned to the judgment-seat. But let us recur to Beethoven's more human suggestion. Fate knocketh in the form of Duty; Promethean free-will, human passion, rebels and struggles for a time, but at last yields; and heroic resolve is triumphant— heroic love. For, "Ach !" methinks these terrible blows are indeed those of Fate ; but also those, viz., which nailed Heroic Love (comprehend both words) to the cross—heroic love that made even

> " Destiny coincide with Choice ;"

--that from the horrible instrument of torture and death itself, cried, " Father ! forgive them, for they know not what they do ;" and in the midst of the greatest of struggles and temptations (viz., with himself), wrestled and conquered, and cried, " Not my will (the local), but Thine (the universal) be done."— Such is the colossal difference between the pictures of Christ submitting, and Prometheus cursing the gods.

It is a remarkable fact, that this symphony is so great—indeed, the greatest; and yet, it is a fact fundamentally, instructively natural; for, not pre-meditating it beforehand, Beethoven sat down to write about the greatest thinkable subject out of his inmost own heart—nay, as it were, with his own heart's blood. Another remarkable fact is, that the so much abused public soon realized that this sym-phony was the greatest. This symphony paints Beethoven's life—especially inner life—which "life" properly means. Here we see genius struggling with fate, in which his life was sunk (like every life); wherewith our little life is rounded, as with a sleep. Fate! What had it done for Beethoven? What does it mean?

In the first place—mysteriously great fact—Fate had from the outset given him her own answer, had put into his hands *the* weapon for defeating her, viz., Genius. Armed with this, he can bide his time, and take all the drawbacks *plus;* especially as with him genius implies, what, properly, it always implies, Valour—or, in the valuable Latin double-sense or many-sense of the word, Virtue. The drawbacks—disagreeables, obstacles, from drunken father, aye, and own character, downward—in no wise fail to come. Amongst the gravest are the physical, deafness; one mixed, unsatisfied heart; and one spiritual, unsatis-fied soul—all sunk in the adamantine environment of Fate. But then, as observed, Fate equips her adversary for the battle. And mark how Beethoven quits himself in the encounter. In early morning, in the burden and heat of the day, and by declining sun, he—like every true man, (like the Son of Man, or Brother of Man)—fights Fate with his life; makes his *life* answer doubts, and queries, and despair, the crucial questions which Fate forces on him. It is in this sense Emerson's saying applies. Beethoven thus answered questions he was not conscious enough to put; as, on the other hand, he also put questions he had not the power to answer—like the nineteenth century itself—questions which the twenty-ninth will probably be seeking a solution for. When Fate buffeted Beethoven at home (bitter mockery!), he worked in the direction, and with the instrument, which nature gave him; when she appeared as grim *Vierge de Fer*, commanding him to earn his bread, he worked; when she appeared (more cruelly) as syren (mocking him), he worked (not went away and rioted); when—the most unkind cut of all—she made him deaf (him, Beethoven the grandest representation of man for the constituency, Music), he worked harder than ever; and all through the time, down to the end, *when* he could not, *though* he could not, satisfy the most irrepressible and unsatisfiable of all inquirers, his own unsettled soul—incapable of *grasping* eternity, *knowing* it must exist; incapable of *proving* immortality, feeling it is the very breath of life and beauty, and must be—from first to last, he worked. For this, he could dispense with going to hear Immanuel Kant; though, assuredly, their understanding of the "Categorical Imperative" was one, viz., Conscience (?). "Two things strike me dumb, —the heavens by night, and the moral law in man." Let Fate knock as she may,—unannounced, her loudest, long-sustained—as in these portentous notes (was ever chord of the dim. 7th so treated—so inspiredly?):—

in these notes—whose indefinite dwelling seems to say, "I pause for a reply." Fate confronts man—a being *repleto di virtù;* a being bound by will, but with an unique sense of freewill : here she meets consciousness-and-conscience. Her blows are hard ; but "a soft answer (the *p* ensuing) turneth away wrath"—Beethoven turns her blows (*her* blows) into beauty. I am also here struck by the reflection, that we may consider these as the blows of death (*cum æquo pede*)—*that* form of fate; and they are answered by the soft whisper—"immortality." This soft whisper rises into storm-loudness, at its grandest (further on), that is, where man cries, "Aye, and though personal immortality be a vain dream, I will be immortal here, and thus answer thee, thou bug-bear, Death ! Suffice it for me to be here great and good !"

Mark especially, somewhat further on, after the stormy passage, the strain in the major (E flat). I have no words for its beauty (especially if played *andante*) ; it is like star-dew fallen into the bosom of a lily. Or, again, "deep answering unto deep," he rises and strikes her back with power. Every depth into which her blows fell him, only confers on this Antæus new power. Though o'er him, in the words of the Greek Beethoven (Aiskulos—in the Greek Macbeth, Agamemnon)—

> "Billow-like, woe rolls on woe,
> In the light of heaven,"

they

> "Cannot bring him wholly under, more
> Than loud south-westerns, rolling ridge on ridge,
> The buoy that rides at sea, and dips and springs
> For ever;"

—to use our own poet's magnificent image—(type, as here applied, of character; or of immortality—the eternal hope of it in man). Such we figure the conduct of this Titan in the stupendous conflict—Titan, who made the very gods tremble :—

> " FIALTE.—La nome; e fece le gran prove,
> Quando i giganti fer paura ai Dei."—

He conquers, because

> " Soleva la lancia
> D'Achille e del suo padre esser cagione
> Prima di triste e poi di buona mancia,"

to quote the *Italian* Beethoven; the spear of Achilles, and his father, heals its wounds. The cruel blows of Fate and Temptation (to error and despair) are resisted, cured, and beaten, as before said, by her own gift, or by herself, in the form of character and genius. In the light of the higher reading before-mentioned, Fate, under the terrible but divine form of duty (divine necessity), knocks at man's heart, and bids it open; but that being human—

> " Frailty, thy name is Man," —

hesitates, protests, rebels, in all the strength of selfish passion, of full-armed nature. As before thrown out, the grand lesson (whatever dialect man may speak or think), the tremendous spectacle, is in the Garden of Gethsemane and in Golgotha. Thither we must repair, if we would realize the force of this idea—of this music. In the light of morning we have once again played it (*gewiss* not like a Rubinstein), and find our words no whit too strong (after orchestral performance one is simply overpowered). We are struck with the impression that it is the most dramatic work, not only in music, but human performance (no painting, even, can so evoke all the feelings of the Cross); and we would use the higher imaginings we have to give our brother musicians an idea of the true greatness, the sacred grandeur, of their art : it knows no rival but poetry.

Let us, then, with a final glance at that stupendous drama, close. Fate, in the thunder-pregnant darkness, over all the cypress-bowers and cedar-glooms, "commends" the fearful chalice to the lips. Ensues the highest of struggles—godlike; but, finally, with the most immortal of earth's words, Character, the softly invincible heroism of self-sacrificing love, the grandeur of filial submission to the Universal Will, conquers ; and a strain of seventh-heaven triumph bears away the words—"FATHER, not my will, but Thine be done !" It is the same in the fell scene of Golgotha. As we said, these blows are the nails driven home ; *but they cannot nail down the spirit;* and the spouting blood is a fountain of glory ; the cross by magic, made the highest symbol of men. Fate may do her worst now—from without or within ; temptation was trampled under foot ; and, lo ! Fate is conquered !—or rather, one with apotheosis and immortality.

The Andante.

I recollect reading, some one exclaimed, in natural rapture on hearing this andante of andantes (the only rival of the sonata theme in A flat—?) "Oh! what must that man have felt who wrote this !" Yes; felt when he wrote it, and all through life. What inner life was not his! " It comes before me," as the Germans say, that this movement should be played before the distant sea, in the westering sun of a summer's day. Methinks, on its heavenliest of dreams, in view of that suggested sea of immortality, Beethoven's own spirit might pass away; had a sanctioned longing so to do; not in misanthropic disgust (nothing Byronic, à la Manfred) but at peace—with all, all. This is the celestial *Nunc Dimittis :* the life and worship, including work, in the temple—this infinite—is over ; the Messiah is come ; higher life dawns upon men—therefore, " Lord, now lettest thou thy servant depart in peace !"

It is impossible to express, only possible in some sort to feel, the unfathomable peace shadowed forth in this music. Or, again, it is a *Kinderscene,* greater than any of any Schumann. As for " Songs without words," they are tinsel to it. Here is a reverie by one of the highest, dearest, of men, from the summit where he first sees his shadow slope towards the grave, back into the holy dreamland of childhood. Here is its mystic infinitude reflected and shadowed forth by a heart that almost dies in the process for yearning and love. *Dies heisst Sehnsucht, dies Liebe !*

If Shakespeare, in his marvellous serenity, implies all the storms fought out beforehand (a description difficult to mend); here we have, at least, "the Peace of God which passeth understanding" (is superior to—as Goethe reads it—as well as, baffles), when they *have* been fought out by the man, the sight of whom struggling with adversity (inner as well as outer, faults of character as well as blows of fate) benefits the gods. Here we have a spirit sunk in such peace as Petrarch's departed Laura speaks of—

" Mio ben non cape in intelletto umano "—

in the sphere Mamiani's "Ithuriel" describes, where there reigns an eternal

> " Santa armonia di voglie e di pensieri"—

sacred harmony of thought and will—which is the eternal desideratum, which so few men have, even the greater ones; sphere wherein our Beethoven himself, that

> " Anima alpestre,"

storm-tossed soul, buffeted spirit, out of harmony with himself and others, did not most reside (Shakespeare, on the contrary, did—seemed a *native* of it, nay, dwelling *in* it, and speaking *thence* of the tragedies and annoys of earth); but of whose profoundest heart in compensation he knew the deepest secret, in whose bosom's centre he nestled (in his happy hours), repairing thither from the disgusts and battles of the world, or expatiating in the blessed hope of everlasting life, after the raging conflict of doubts and queries, to whose inmost holy of holies he penetrated, and was welcomed; he, the wayward child—to extend the idea—leaving all his toys, and running in a passion of sobs to the Eternal Bosom, with a more peculiar smile than that other who dwelt for ever in its courts, or lingered round his mother's (the Madonna's) knee; for Mozart I fancy the Mother's favourite, Beethoven the Father's; o'er Mozart's music one would inscribe this—

> " Madre, fonte d'amore
> Ove ogni odio s'ammorza
> Che su dal ciel tanta dolcezza stilie,

but over Beethoven's—

> " Ma sovra Olimpo ed Ossa
> Trona il gran Giove."

Here, in this andante of andantes, we have, as in the bosom of spring after the storms of winter—as over cerulean seas in a southern clime after them,—that effluence, which is like the satisfaction of a good conscience; that breath which went up from the dominated ocean, when One said—"Be Still!"

THE ALLEGRO.

" Quando Giove fu arcanamente giusto."
" Ich glaube, nur Gott versteht unser Musik."

These two mottoes, from Dante and Jean Paul, give some sort of expression to the feelings excited by this music—music which makes rather premature that offer of a premium for a new epithet, at Symphony, No. 2. And yet it is distinctly the same Beethoven here, only full grown; not only serpent-strangling, but hydra-killing and labour-doing Hercules. Jove, left for ever the society of the nymphs, and speaking from the central throne, *orcanamente giusto*. One is certain, Beethoven himself could not have *explained* this music; there is such a mysterious pregnancy in it, such a holy ominousness (if not played too fast), such a shadowy sorrow, such other-world tones of pathos and resolution and triumph. This is a message the prophet does not dream of daring to try and comprehend; an utterance which the oracle itself would never attempt to explain. This is the sort of music Jean Paul alluded to, when he declared that it was above our own understanding, clear only to the Divine. This is the sort of music which might illustrate his sublime utterance, " Women are beautiful, because they suffer so much." Here (once more), we have the Invisible Host chaunting in almost appalling mournfulness round the cross, or the tomb—"It is over; it is over. The Man of Sorrows, and acquainted with grief! Thus have they 'done to death' their Highest among them!" But then—

ensues such high retrospect and encouragement—

" Love bears it out even to the end of doom ;"

then such angelic clamour of triumph—"O grave, where is thy victory! O death, where is thy sting?" This, too, is a walk "over the field of battle by night" (Marx, *re* the Funeral March, *Eroica*); but it is another battle-field than a Napoleonic one—the world is the field, and Heroic Love has gone down on it, like a cloven star at sea. The world is the field, and the highest and the lowest in us doing battle therein, amidst heaps of slain. Poor humanity!

It has been a fearful conflict. What do we not deplore? But, lo! as the infernal volumes roll sluggishly away, as though loth to quit the hateful banquet, high above all an unspeakable orb shines through, the orb of promise and peace. "Ach!" poor man, there is enough, indeed, to root pessimism in thee; evil seems to have nestled in every pore; life seems to try how hard she can make it to live; thou thyself shudderest at thy self; art tortured by appetites, goaded by passions, infested by thoughts, distracted by doubts, almost driven to despair. But, no! do *not* despair. Progress is slow, but sure. All is justified at last; and higher life lightens in the dawn. Nay, even if thy dearest hope be a dream—that word too great for any mouth, Immortality—be good (great and strong) *here; that,* if not so happy, is a still higher immortality—

> "Then what could death do, if thou should'st depart,
> Leaving thee living in posterity?"

In such a sea of thoughts—such a thousand-path'd forest—does Beethoven's music plunge us; such a branching piece of the Infinite is it. For the rest, apart from ideas and images, the mere notes have an eternal self-charm. Who fore-ordered this collocation and sequence? Who suggested these harmonious mysteries? How minor and major here phrase and fall together! Never did they do so before; rarely will they do so again. Beethoven was a divine kaleidoscope in a divine hand.

The *fugato* page takes us into another order of ideas. Here it would almost seem as though tragedy, which threatened to take entire possession of the spirits, were shaken off, and cheerful activity resumed. Here we seem to have the chase, or a military *festival,* or the resolute alacrity which precedes a patriotic war. The climax, those *klingende* concords, in C *alt.,* are very fresh and brilliant; and the imitation is a very interesting characteristic bit of Beethoven (proof amongst many that he studied Handel, if he studied anybody); nevertheless, though the resumption of the original inspired motive is simply grand (peculiar to Beethoven), a slightly uncomfortable feeling is occasioned by this music, in juxtaposition with its predecessor. A certain violence seems done to us; we feel "Is not this rather an incongruous intercalation?" Contrast it certainly is, and excellent in itself; but, had it not been better to have left it out altogether? nay, to have been content with the wonderful allegro as it stood—in those continent bars sublime, and not to be eclipsed. Are we not here too suddenly transported from sub-tropical to temperate zone; or, rather, from some undiscovered inter-world, where is the highest discourse on the

"Issues of Life and Death"

to every-day life? In any case, the music is curiously lighter than the preceding; nay, almost suggests the thought that Beethoven might have here made use of a more youthful idea. And, in strict justice, we must say, it is below the level—if not, indeed, unworthy of, incompatible with, this stupendous symphony. In one word, it does not seem to exist of inner neces-sity (the eternal test), like its marvellous predecessor : it was written, but not inspired.

THE FINALE.

This, rather than, as Marx says, the last movement of Symphony No. 2, might be designated the finale of finales (?)—"The most sublime chaunt of triumph ever pealed forth by an orchestra." *Multum in parvo* I have put a mark against the D, because that one touch (of nature) makes all the difference ; nay, I had almost said, stamps the passage. Substitute a B, and the emphasis is lost, together with the originality. Nevertheless, the movement is hardly of equal value throughout ; it has its "worser half;" and is also, unfortunately, too long. As in so many other cases, ideas are repeated, repeated already. But this is not the worst; the worst is, that the overwhelming effect of the stupendous burst is seriously impaired. It should have

> "Smitten once, to smite no more."

This terrible "elaboration," so superfluously "necessary"; such a fancied *sine quâ non!* Here, we must seriously repeat the protest against the conventional custom; nay, almost raise the question, whether it is not rather a reproach to Beethoven (the original) that he did not get out of this thoughtless old groove. Here, the idea did not extrude the form, but rather *con*formed to it; was, as it were, poured into the traditional mould. But the form should be the eventuation of the idea, of the germ-soul ("*pensiero di Dio*"), as in a living organism (tree, *e.g.*, or man).* With regard to the "worser half" we ventured to speak of, it is simply, as in so many cases, even in Beethoven himself, and notably (as we have so often felt) in the *Lieder ohne Worte;* there, very rarely is the second motive equal to the first; the first *was* motive — the "germ-soul," inner necessity of the piece, *perforce* giving birth to it; the second was factitious. In the present case, does not this subject—

---

* Neither can we but regret the re-introduction of the "allegro" subject; that sublime idea had already done its true work (as we feel), and there only remained to break into one overwhelming burst of triumph, and then an end.

seem really trifling (nay, almost jiggy) by the side of the grand opening, so broad and victorious? We are rather reminded of that traditional movement, whose ambling hilarity is our special horror, viz., the Rondo —we hope by now decently dead and buried ; nay, we think, too, of the Sonata in G (Op. 31). This unlucky subject seems to us as unworthy its glorious predecessor as the last movement of that sonata is unworthy of the first—that burst of inspiration, like water from the rock, rolling on into broad *Symphonische Dichtung.* (In the course of the present *motiv*, consecutive octaves are prominent). A little further on—one bar and a half, true Beethoven, is worth a page of such undignified *Tonspiel.* It is one of those bars which convey a "shock of delight" whenever they catch the musician's eye—

Few pleasures could be more elegant than to extend such an idea *ad lib.* as an andante on the organ. (We can imagine its effect as a prelude in some old rural church—say on a mellow Sunday afternoon).

Another notable point is, the " grinding out" (long before Berlioz) of the minor second against the tonic ; an effect of extraordinary resolution and power—

eloquently expressive, indeed, of a determination to

bear it out against the shocks of doom. In this and other traits, we have the true Beethoven—such spiritual energy as (except in Handel, and with him it was less human) had not yet been dreamt of; such suffering in strife, and yet such glorying in it; such temptations in the wilderness (of his own heart, as well as elsewhere); such final victorious success! And, here we are brought back into our old more genial vein and strain; we forget the spots on the sun, and lose ourselves in his overpowering effulgence. This "*erhabensten Triumphgesang*" is, to us, that of resurrection; when the ponderous lid was burst from within with light, which at once—so the great fancy expatiates—redoubled the splendour of day all over the world. Handel's selected words—nay, and very remarkably, the great flash-of-chorus itself (one could, indeed, imagine it as having suggested Beethoven's, they are so much alike)—come into the mind,—

"By Man came also the Resurrection of the Dead."

And these—

"LA RISURREZIONE.

"Viva l'eterno Dio: sconfilto e vinto
D'Averno il crudo regnator sen giace:
L'empio pur sente il fiero braccio avvinte,
E l'aspra morte abbassa il ciglio, e tace.
Cade all'uom la catena onde fu cinto
Per fallo antico di pensiero audace:
Iddio, dell'uom vendicatore ha vinto!
Il ciel canta vittoria, e annunzia pace.
Io veggo gia sovra l'eterea mole
Erger di Croce trionfale insegna,

Primo terror d'ogni tartarea trama.
E veggo in alto soglio il sommo Sole,
Che a regnare in eterno ov'egli regna
I redenti mortali aspetta, e chiama."

In Teutonic language, which finds in the highest imaginings only the symbol and apotheosis of human worth and endeavour ; which believes, indeed, that by man came and comes the resurrection from the dead ; and which regards that life as the most priceless page in human history, to be for ever applied and interpreted by sympathy at will; and first becoming truly divine when we regard it as truly human—in Teutonic thought and dialect, we will conclude with this eloquent and intrinsic application to the greatest of Beethoven's symphonies :—" Nohl names the work the musical Faust of the moral will and its conflicts; a work whose progress shows that there is something greater than Fate, namely, Man, who, descending into the abysses of his own self, fetches counsel and power wherewith to battle with life ; and then, re-inforced through his conviction of indestructible oneness with the god-like, celebrates, with dythyrambic victory, the triumph of the eternal Good, and of his own inner Freedom."

The Pastoral Symphony, No. VI, Op. 68.

" Here (in Heiligenstadt, near Vienna, in the summer of 1808, lying by the brook with nut-trees, listening to the birds singing), I wrote the ' Scene by the Brook,' and the goldhammers there up above me, the quails and cuckoos round about me, helped compose."—Beethoven to Schindler. These last words throw a light on the oft-abused passage where the birds are imitated. We should not judge a Beethoven hastily—especially not assign to his action low grounds. We here see that the passage was not introduced in mere material imitation, but rather as a genial tribute and record ; *so* the passage becomes beautiful, and the opposite of superficial. Emerson says, " Yon swallow weaving his straw into his nest should weave it into my poem." No doubt, in the savage—in his passionate love of freedom and roaming—we already find the germ of the poetic love of nature ; and some two thousand years ago we find such sublime celebration as this (and what ages of evolution does it imply !)—

> " As when in heaven the stars about the morn
> Look beautiful, when all the winds are laid,
> And every height comes out and jutting peak
> And valley, and the immeasurable heavens
> Break open to their highest."—Iliad (Tennyson).

> " A rock-wall'd glen, water'd by a streamlet,
> And shadowed o'er with pines."—Euripides (Milman).

> " Yon starry conclave
> Those glorious dynasts of the sky, that bear
> Winter and summer round to mortal man."
> —Aiskulos (Idem).

> " Smooth lies the surface of the purple seas,
> Nor curl'd, nor whiten'd, by the gentle breeze ;
> No more, hoarse dashing from the breakers steep,
> The heavy waves recoil into the deep ;
> The zephyrs breathe, the murm'ring swallow weaves
> Her straw-built chamber 'neath the shadowy eaves."
> —Agathias (Idem).

And yesterday, was written—

> " Vesuvius wears his brilliant plume
> Above a sun-lit dome of snow ;
> And darkly thro' the illumin'd gloom
> Extends his mighty base below :

On Mount St. Angelo's ponderous crest,
  And in his furrows, snow, too, sleeps ;
Great glitt'ring clouds are piled o'er that :
  All rises out of glamourous deeps ;

For, glinting up, thro' olive bowers,
  And many an arm-outstretching tree,
Is the sun-tipt, early-winter-morning,
  Slumberous, breathing sea."

In the sister arts—sister graces—painting and music,
down to Turner and the Turner of music, Beethoven
(he also would have given us the Python slaying
Apollo, and the going home of the Téméraire, the
Plague of Darkness, Æneas leaving Carthage, and
Italy, Ancient and Modern : Schumann, too, is very
Turner-like, perhaps more so, has more of that mystical glamour—Beethoven, like Rembrandt, only
ideal) ; in the sister arts, Nature could not fail to be
celebrated, or rather let us say ideally reproduced,
and even transfigured, through the geniuses of these
arts, her eldest children—nay, herself (made man).
In Beethoven, then—a tone-poet, German, and *born
on the Rhine*, at, perhaps, its grandest part—as we
might expect, this worship and celebration of nature,
this apotheosis in tone, culminates. Her sweetness
and her grandeur, coloured, too, by his own Beetho-
ven-soul, are by him sublimely revealed—in many a
page and passage dear to the sympathetic knower.
It was, then, impossible that Beethoven should *not*
write (betitled or not) a Pastoral Symphony; and this,
if only as one manifestation of his (like nature) many-
sidedness. Moreover, though the Greek poesy reads
as fresh as if written yesterday, nevertheless nature-
worship, such as we understand it—an overpowering
sense of her mysticism, a rapturous *losing* of ourselves
in her—seems a thing not only specially Teutonic and

modern, but modern even among the Teutonic peoples themselves, dating after the Reformation; and, indeed, almost as though nature-worship was to supply the place of religion (in the narrow sense, worship of an anthropomorphic maker of nature), rapture in her to supply the place of religious rapture, no longer possible; if so, a beautiful ordinance! Hence, then, if we go a little way below the surface, the present masterpiece, Beethoven's universally favourite (though far from greatest, indeed, the Symphony in D is superior—much more powerful, especially the first movement, and at least equally fresh) " Pastoral Symphony." It does not, indeed (at least the opening allegro), celebrate that peculiar, that sacred sentiment we have been speaking of; it does not utter the unutterable, but it is a true and lovely nature-poem nevertheless, worthy of all acceptation; without it the splendid series of symphonies would have been incomplete. Let us approach it.

What STRIKES us in this "household-word" work, especially in the first movement, is its significant simplicity. It is wonderful, as revealing to us how *profoundly* simple a great man can be, and is; sublime in that, as well as in his opulence and power; indeed, simplicity is an inevitable concomitant and *sine quâ non* of power; even in a Napoleon, let alone a Shakespeare, a Newton, and a Beethoven.

So simple is the allegro, that it almost seems studiously so—almost as though Beethoven thereby wished to convey a reproach, at least a monition, to the artificial, and said, "Thus I hold the mirror up to Nature!" Musically, the piece (as it has always seemed to us) rather suffers by this. The ideas are more than usually re-repeated; and, remarkably, re-

iterations (though perhaps there was a psychological
reason for this in the soul of Beethoven, as instinc-
tively expressive, over and over again, of the one
great joy he felt, or as saying—"After all, the essence
and compelling spirit of this great Nature is one").
Moreover, the ideas, though in themselves beautifully
pure and characteristic, seem almost *too* simple, nay
we had almost said languid, for they rather suggest
to us the gratification of a convalescent than of a
passionately profound (aye, and profoundly passionate) lover of nature, such as all Germans are, such as
Schumann intensely was, and such as Beethoven must
have exceptionally been. (Brendel says, Haydn's
love of nature, as revealed in his music, was that of
her very child, unconscious; Beethoven's, that of a
town-dweller, conscious. But to this I would reply,
town-dweller by compulsion). On the other hand, if
Beethoven wished to enter a protest against *Schwär-*
merei, for nature, none could be more effective than
this movement. But nature ever was and remains
mystic, and no celebration of her, above all by a
Beethoven, can satisfy us which does not shadow
forth, is not overpowered by, a sense of this—sense
peculiar to this latter age; more so, even, than the
similar companion-sense of love. Love without
Schwärmerei were not love; no more is love of
nature. For these profounder realizations of nature,
" glances into the deepest deeps of beauty," (Carlyle,
on the remark about "the lilies of the field") reflected adumbrations of her wizardry, a sense of her
intoxicating aroma, the ecstasy in her bosom, that
mesmerizing infinitude of hers, we must look to Beethoven's sonatas, or other portions of his symphonies;
and to such music as Schumann's; hardly in his Pastoral Symphony (except somewhat in the andante);

more in his Pastoral Sonata—*that* first movement is *profound*, as well as richer. There we see the poet-philosopher, nay, high-priest of nature; and the movement, four-square, almost perfect, is one of the masterpieces, and most precious legacies of Nature's Eldest Child. In the present movement we have peaceful pleasure, but not rapture, if even joy, or delight (in the Sonata Pastorale we have contemplative joy)—though Beethoven may possibly have expressly chastened the expression of feeling, as being, so, more "pastoral." Be that as it may, here we have sweetness rather than power (except, indeed, behind all); nay, rather the gratification of an habitual dweller in the country (and he no longer a young man), than the burst of rapture we might have expected from a lover of nature only just let loose from town. However, Beethoven *has* written over the movements—"*Awakening* of cheerful emotions on arrival in the country." He further said, the symphony was feeling rather than painting. This is a matter of course from a Beethoven ; and note, it is a Beethoven's feelings that are depicted. What we have in the work is Nature *plus* Beethoven—nature photographed after passing through him, and so becoming idealised. We have, however, both scene-painting and soul-painting through the emotions here excited and described ; we see also the landscape which to a great extent occasioned them ; (thus, this, like Goethe's, is an occasional poem). It is a truly pastoral district; quiet, sunny scenery, with a scent of the earliest hay ; but nature in her splendour, with, say, in the distance, the great sea ; nature, a blaze of flowers embosomed in hills, as in our own beautiful England in May ; let alone nature in spring, with her background of Alps and Appenines. Nature, whose

greatest hint—the secret of whose greatest power is,
Immortality ; a promise of that is hardly here celebrated ; or, rather, that hint is not, for it is in every
landscape :—"I, too, have looked upon the hills in
their hazy veil, but their greatest charm, to me, was
their promise."   Neither, in spite of Elterlein's
charming allusion, have we the scenery where, or the
time when (*soust*) as Goethe so truly, sublimely ex-
presses it (in two of his most inspired lines)—

> "*Stürzte* sich der Himmelsliebe Kuss
> Auf mich herab in ernsber Sabbath stille."

When Beethoven wrote this music he had not in
mind his revered Shakespeare's magnificent—

> " Full many a glorious morning have I seen
> Flatter the mountain-tops with sovereign eye,
> Kissing with golden face the meadows green,
> Gilding pale streams with heaving alchemy."

This, rather, the immortal Symphony in A suggests ;
or such lines as these :—

> " My other mighty passion was for thee,
> Thou glimmering, glamouring, manifestation of God !
> Unspeakable Nature, with thy distant sea,
> Wave-framing hills, dim woods, and flowery sod ;
> My haziest, sweetest memories, are of you,
> Where inland-county beauty guards its stream ;
> Oh ! ' violet ' memory ' dim ' with *my* tears' dew ;
> Oh ! shadowy pausing, touch'd with earliest beam ;
> And sea-side recollections stir my heart,
> The calm's majestic cheerfulness, the storm,
> The bluff that through the vapours seem'd to start,
> A thousand miracles of tint and form ;
> And ever as I yearn'd on wave and hill,
> The unconscious secret was thy Promise still."

The " Scene by the Brook "—

> " I draw them all along, and flow
> To join the brimming river ;
> Men may come and men may go,
> But I go on for ever."

(exquisite image of immortality bearing along mortality)—is richer in significance. There, indeed, we do get some of those deep glimpses, far glances (and tender ones into flower-cups)—those unspeakable hints (note especially, as usual, the passage in the extra-poetic key of G flat; where, however, also as usual, Beethoven lingers too little; indeed, even he seems rather to *deviate* into such keys, and to be afraid of dwelling in them). We see Beethoven, the colossally *un*happy soul, here at least happy, nay, blessed; lapped in flowers; caressed by the stream; soothed and tended by all the "angels and ministers of grace" of nature; while the everlasting heaven pronounces its benediction over him.

For our own part, we are specially affected, because we call to mind a brook where we also were wont to be happy. But, it was not in quiet scenery, but in a Swiss mountain-valley; the brook came from heaven, and coursed through pine-woods and pastures into a stupendously beautiful lake, the shadows of whose mighty guardian Alps are reflected also in the Moonlight Sonata; while, afar off, as it were in colossal admonition, towered those eternal reminders, the peaks of the Bernese Oberland.

The Scherzo has always seemed to us an inspiration—as much as the storm; so original and powerful, so tuneful in its picturesque, spontaneous gaiety. It is Beethoven at his genialist. The sublimity of the storm may speak for itself: I will only remark, in reply to the German Hume, who rather cavils and carps, and is no Beethoven-worshipper (but Mozart), and says "the cause for such a very loud storm is too trifling"—that the storm *also* perchance broke over crowned heads and the fate of empires (Napoleon died in a storm, and so, just as curiously charac-

teristic, did Beethoven).   Storms do, too, come up
in the brightest summer day (without or within us);
and, in short, though the criticism is truly philosophical, that it should be left doubtful whether the
storm was a physical or moral one—of nature or
human nature—Beethoven, as ever, is entitled to a
genial interpretation, a liberal application.   In the
meanwhile, *as* a storm—storm of music, as well as
musical storm—it is as grand as original; shaking us
with the fullness of those sublime emotions of the
natural storm (and surely our German Hume would
not disparage these!), and its introduction is a happy
felicity.

Beethoven's "Lobgesang," which concludes the
work, is very noble in its unstudied beauty, expressing "pious and grateful feelings" by unsophisticated
men after storm.   The treatment of the greatly-
simple theme is a masterpiece and model.   Here is
Wagner anticipated, but not spoilt!   To sum up:
the first movement, very exceptionally, is the weakest
of all; and the whole work, though a treasure of its
own, coming from Beethoven, revealing him as singularly loveable, is in no way so surpassing as to
preclude the attempt by a follower also to compose
a Pastoral Symphony.   We conclude with Herr
Elterlein's summary of the work— very charming,
although he finds in the allegro considerably more
than we do.

"A refreshing morning breeze greets us; we
have left behind the crowds and walls of the town.
We are in the mood of Faust, on the sunny Easter
spring morning.   At first we are in silent rapture, the
climax is not yet reached, Nature's myriad living
voices do not at once re-echo in our inmost spirit.
The farther we wander, the more natural beauties

open up and greet us, the more multifarious becomes the scene. In proportion as the variety becomes richer, and the impression of this divine beauty— (*Gottesnatur*—German ought to be *known by every musician*, and read in the original, because their pregnant, often pantheistic, shades of expression, become lost in English ; or, if 'transcribed,' are 'not English ')—deeper, the more our rapture swells to utmost joy. Now, we perfectly revel (*schwelgen ganz*) in the full feast ; entirely abandon ourselves to the impressions of absolute Nature ; completely at one with ourselves, in this kingdom, we feel ourselves at one with her.

" We have now reached the acmé of enthusiasm ; our soul trembles in silent ecstasy ; involuntarily the desire awakes in us, after expatiating in the universal beauty of Nature, to contemplate and enjoy her still life and operations in intimate communion.

" Therefore, the scene changes in the second movement. We are transplanted to a peaceful woodland vale, through which a brook babbles. ' *Scene am Bach*,' the tone-picture is also called by the master ; it is elaborated out in the most thoughtful manner, and displays before us, in the richest, fullest colours, the murmur of the brook, the rustling of the swayed tree-tops, and the song of the birds. At last the brook is still, the trees rustle no more ; we have already once said farewell to the soft babbling that long kept us spell-bound—quail, cuckoo, and nightingale are alone still heard.—(Beautifully imagined ! as it were, also saying 'farewell' to the sympathetic wanderer up the vale ; who, only another human form of them, had stayed so long with them, loving them like their brother, enchanted by their song— enchanted in Nature's bosom. This way of putting it (of receiving it) is only another proof of the non-materialism, non-superficialism, nay, of the beauty of this passage (withal, quite brief—*only introduced at the end*) ; and a proof of the value and necessity of sympathetic audition of a Beethoven's works. Only a poet—never Dryasdust—can rightly criticise a poet).

"In the third movement the scene is again changed. We find ourselves in meadows. The characteristic multiformity of this piece would have told us its meaning, without the master's words. So, too, the storm—those tones full of fearful, dark sublimity. At last, the tempest and its fury cease, only in the distance the thunder still growls ; the blue sky again opens up, the evening sun casts its mild light o'er the landscape—(genial thought)—enlivened by shepherds whose shalm now sounds.

"The fourth movement, therefore, is dedicated to ' Shepherd's Song,'—' pious and grateful feelings after the storm.' The grateful strains begin softly, then swell ever more and more to topmost joy, pouring forth at their climax an intense, solemn, and yet again such a plain, simple thank-offering to Nature's Creator."

SYMPHONY, No. 7, Op. 92.

In this magnificent symphony, the most picturesque of all, Beethoven seemed to have taken a new lease of originality. It is specially instructive and encouraging on that account; and, amongst other evidences, makes us weigh, whether his "third manner" (whereof this may be considered the noble isthmus that joins those continents), was really progress or decay, or a dubious transition step to something higher. However, the work is reckoned among those of his second manner, and so is certainly a potent argument for those who,

with enlightened honesty (and not Philistine blindness), feel that Beethoven's second style is, *par excellence,* Beethoven—whether Wagner began or not
where Beethoven left off. *Apropos* of Wagner, does
not this "Poco Sostenuto" call to mind that Wizard
of the South's famous morçeaux in "Lohengrin," in
the same key? Is not the style—nay, the motiv—
much the same ?—

There seems something of the same *mysticism,* though
Beethoven is not tainted with the morbidness one
scents in Wagner; seems, as a whole, broader, nobler,
more *natural,* more truly deep; in a word, more
healthy, and therefore greater, notwithstanding Wagner's undoubted genius, and still more stupendous
energy for which we most envy him. This opening
theme has a powerful tranquility about it—like that,
say, of some Epaminondas : seems, as it were, an
assurance and announcement that Beneficence, at
bottom and after all, is paramount in this stupendous
paradox and discrepancy called the universe ; notwithstanding, it seems to go on to say, the ground-bass
of storm, on and over which true heroism will ever
ride (*re-entry of the theme ff*); notwithstanding the
painfulnesses, which are only subtler proofs and
manifestations of self-justified righteousness and
power—most sublime in its subtlest judgments—as
the private life of every self-strict person knows.
Then, a new theme—fragment of the same essential
peace—enters ; curiously (and beautifully) reminding
us of that early, early work of Beethoven's (Oh,

Rhine-lad, written *how* long ago !), the Sonata in C
dedicated to Haydn—

but gaining by being slow.

But " action, action, action," which these climbing
basses—("And ever climbing up the climbing wave"),
"life is painfully real,"—seem to say, soon break in
again on this Elysian dream.   It re-appears, however, like a heavenly messenger, holding us spell-
bound, in a trance or veritable dream, whereof these
two conflicting elements form the chief apparitions ;
conflicting, yet viewed largely, harmonious, like their
counterparts in that oneness,   Life,—whose painfulnesses are as much a *necessary* part of it, as discords
are of entire music.

The Vivace.

Great pictures—pictures of great action (like the
actions themselves)—represent the moral qualities
behind.   Hence, many a page of music, eminently of
Beethoven, may be objectively or subjectively interpreted, or both.   It is the usual practice, and a
natural one, to regard the " Eroica " symphony as
objective, and the C minor as subjective—both illustrating the grand abstract fact, Conflict.   The *vivace*
of the A major symphony *strikes*, no less, as objective.
There is a ringing cheerfulness about it that suggests
no spiritual struggles, psychological battle, but the
open air and its beloved objects—by no means
excluding the world's great foreground feature, man ;

rather, pre-eminently presenting and illustrating him, and this from your Beethoven, the intensely subjective soul. Intensely subjective, yes ! far more so,—more grandly so,—than your Byron ; more *characteristically* so than Shakespeare ; but, nevertheless—nay, therefore—also more truly, nobly objective than the former, kin with the latter (Turner is greater than Rosa).

It is impossible to overstate the bright, the exhilarating impression of these tones. Here we at once revel in the outer world, in all the

April of its prime,

and feel ourselves magically strung up to virile deeds, to face the " rugged Hyrcanian boar "—" to do or die." Here the ringing woodland of feudal times is around us, and all the panoply, pride, pomp, and circumstance of a royal chase. The motto of Stephen Heller's admirable " Chasse " was very apt, which records how the French monarch, plunged in gloom by the death of his beloved, seeks distraction in the chase. Sir Walter—of our erst beloved " Ivanhoe"—comes sweeping through the mind ; a rush of joy almost to tears. We see Garth, born thrall of Cedric, and the Jester in the gladed woodland ; and there, at the glittering jousts (even more so) the heavenly Rebecca, Rowena, the Hero, and the Knight Templar ; Jew and Christian ; plumèd knight and lovely dame. This music is Ivanhoe, not forgetting the glamour of the Crusades, with knight and Saracen, and the breath of the Holy Land through it. Here is the chivalry of warriors, who fought for the Cross ; in an age—so different from ours—when there was a frenzy of belief (thus we be-soul our objective) ; here is a phalanx of Bayards *sans peur et sans reproche*, inflamed with passion of

7

hatred and love, *en route* to storm their way to Calvary. This is the picture to fill our mind with; though we may also think of this glorious music as painting forth the Conqueror William, breaking up the chase to invade Harold's England, as being rock'd over thither on crisp seas in knight-throng'd vessels, gallant with streaming pennon; though we may also think of Ferdinand going out to welcome Columbus (in our copy, at the passage in G minor we have ejaculated, "Our Columbus"—Beethoven!— "has found a New World"), of Cortes and Pizarro invading Mexico (copper-coloured men and tropical scenery we may also conjure up); or, again, of Philip and his pompous Armada—of Elizabeth and English chivalry preparing to greet him. But that picture of the Crusades best suits us. So our nothing-if-not-religious Beethoven, the glorious genius, in the name of music, whose High Priest he was (and whom other great spirits serve), concerned only to pour forth what streamed into him; or rather, concerned only to let it stream through him (for it is certain he did not intentionally celebrate and pourtray all that his mighty music suggests, however the Germans may stamp it as Intellectual Music, *die Musik des Geistes*), so our hardly-entreated, much-bound, but triumphant immortal shadowed forth, on canvas made of air, pictures surpassing Angelo and Raphael—pictures that only a painter-Shakespeare could surpass or rival—pictures that have the material splendour and *éclat* of a Rubens, the intense originality of a Rembrandt, *plus* a *soul* behind and within them, which only higher spirits than they can glimmeringly reveal. We have but to repeat, that these tone-pictures have always a charm *plus* (or even apart from), viz., that of the tones themselves.

Our interpretation of this master-movement is the same as that of Marx Nohl and Elterlein (whom we should *like* to quote at length). Wagner's idea, genially understood, is also acceptable. That gifted despot "finds in the Symphony the apotheosis of the Dance *der in Tönen idealisch verkörperten Leibes bewegung.*" Yes, it is a dance that sings ; high dance and song together, as at some Pindar-celebrated Festival of Apollo ; nay, of some ideal, some skylark soul of joy, not so much convinced of, as absolute lyrical part of, and one with the All ; and threatening to melt for very rapture in its bosom. The Dance !—that is applicable enough, too ! What a majestic *pas de deux* is this ever advancing and retiring Day and Night ! What a stately minuet the Four Seasons ! The river dances to the sea ; the blood (of the lover-poet) dances in the veins ; what a wild waltz of elements we have !—galop of the north wind ; the very sea as it were dances in prolonged rhythmic sway, "*molto maestoso,*" to the all-compelling moon ; nay, the moon and stars themselves, with stupendous majesty " keep time " to their " music of the spheres " through space ; and the great rhythm of obedience — action and re-action, attraction and repulsion—is the grand universal law.

Such are some of the lessons and suggestions of this curiously happy, magnificently pregnant rhythmic movement of Beethoven's ; his first great performance in his new lease of originality—great step on the new road to immortality. The motive itself, truly a motive, is as exquisitely tuneful and simple (how great was Beethoven in not straining after effect !) as *grossartig*; and, *en passant*, it has only to be compared for our instruction for one moment with Mendelssohn's " Song without words."

"The Chase," in the same key and time, Book I, to show the *striking* superiority of Beethoven ; nay, their generic difference—Mendelssohn was talent, and Beethoven genius.   The grandiose breadth, the un-studied inspiration (cause of the former) is essentially, fatally absent in Mendelssohn, say what his fascinated devotees may !   It is with him almost all talent and fancy, not oracle and prophecy.   He is only a nephew of Beethoven's, Schumann his "well-beloved" son (as Wagner is of Schumann).

I should be wrong not to give some of Herr Elterlein's ideas.   After citing Wagner's notion, and repudiating it (naturally enough, unless one gives due weight to the word apotheosis, and due interpretation to the word dance), he alludes to (and also rejects as premature) the notion of Alberti, and others, that the symphony is an "announcement of German triumph and enthusiasm at their freedom at length from the French yoke."   He then says, "Marx and Nohl seem to us to come nearer the truth, when the former finds embodied in the symphony the life of a southern people, especially of the Moorish race in ancient Spain,"—(picturesquely suggestive this ; only does not the key-colouring seem rather too cool ? have we not Teutonic brilliance rather than Oriental ?) —"and the latter" (Herr Dr. Nohl), "*ritterliche Fest-pracht* in general (the festival splendour of chivalry). He continues : —"We also, the more and more pro-foundly we have entered into this creation, have be-come clearer convinced, that, as in the "Eroica," we have displayed political heroism, battling and victo-rious ; in the C minor symphony, the moral conflicts and triumphs of man ; so in the A major symphony, we behold the manifold life and phenomena (*Lebens-strömungen*) of a chivalrous, imaginative, hot-blooded people, in the full enjoyment of their health and power. We fancy one might prefix Goethe's words—

"*Im* vollgewühl, im lebensregen Drange
Vermischte sich die thätige Völkerschaar."

("In lusty swarms, crowds full of life,
The deedful peoples intermixed.")

"To arms! is now the word—arms and harness; and forwards to the peaceful jousts in the fair land. And now, how all hearts at first lightly thrill! then pulses beat ever higher; the crowds muster; the warrior horsemen curvet and gambol on slender steeds; pennons glitter, armour dazzles, swords flash in the sun; and the motley swarms stream forth pell-mell, not to bloody battle, like the hero-spirits of the "Eroica,"—no, but the peaceful tournament!"

The scherzo and finale ("a sort of Bacchus triumph" —?) we shall abstain from discussing (they are of much less intrinsic import than the first two movements); but conclude with a glance at the greatest movement of all (with creditable and instinctive instinct almost always redemanded) the allegretto; first, however, citing two remarkable passages from the finale, worthy the attention of those correspondents of the *Musical Standard* on " False Notation," especially of that one "whose memory could not serve him whether such a passage occurred in the masters":—

This repeatedly and persistently occurs; and it would have been gratifying had Beethoven indicated what he meant by it:—" Bacchusfest ?"—or something deeper? The other passage is curiously like the one ventured by Dr. Macfarren's criticiser. The venture was no doubt perfectly justifiable—almost everything is allowable in music, for deliberate poetic effect.

Beethoven no doubt did it for the sake of intensity.

[P.S.—Since writing the above we have come across a chance remark of Goethe's, which struck us as singularly applicable to this great picturesque symphony. During the campaign in France, he noticed in one of the old German towns, the living contrast of knighthood and monkhood (or chivalry and the cloister, we might say). The suggestive words set us thinking if they might not prompt a symphony; and soon after, we saw that they may be applied, perhaps with curious felicity, to Beethoven's A major. Have we not here, indeed, an epitome of the olden time, with its knights, monks, revels, and all?]

THE ALLEGRETTO.

This has been well called "the riddle of the symphony; nor can we altogether accept Herr Elter-

lein's solution of it, though *geistreich*. He prolongs
his fancy, and looks upon this music as a contagious
pause and period of melancholy, of pathetic reminiscence in the "hot-blooded southern folk." Imaginative sympathy has a right to its own fancies, and
these fancies will ever be more or less true ; nevertheless, a more profound, more sacred gloom—mystery
of sorrow—is borne in upon us in these unfathomable
tones. Here we seem to have the portentous, almost
God-accusing, grief of insane love and virtue, in this
fate-and-madness-haunted world—of Juliet in the tomb
(re-read the tremendous lines)—of the ineffable Ophelia,
after outraged princeliness and intellect had lost its
reason, and killed Ophelia's own venerable father ;—
"Ach !" previous to the violent death (her own) of
an angel. Or, we might feel here the incipient
atheism of a Hamlet himself; wrestling with it, but
dreading he wrestles in vain. Later, it is true (the
A major melody—"immortal" Berlioz calls it), solace
descends from heaven, through the toppling sun-gilt
clouds ; but it is unavailing (indeed, we rather regret
the introduction of this episode ? we had liefer be
plunged to, and remain in, the heart of this " deeper,
and decper still" of grief): Rachel will not be
comforted, in her *sublime* despair ; and the final
strains seem those of incurable, illimitable woe. Ah !
these are the strains, too, the accents—" Oh, Jerusalem, Jerusalem ! thou that killest the prophets, how
often would I have gathered thee as a hen gathereth
her chickens and thou wouldst not !" The divine
resolution to sacrifice self for all that (the A major
motive ?) remains even firmer, but the divine sorrow
at it remains even deeper and inextinguishable.

SYMPHONY No. 8.　OP. 93.

Man divides his time chiefly between love (of all sorts) and action. One of his most passionate, as well as purest, loves, is of nature. When the two blend—when at once the lover, and lover of nature, roams in nature, besouling and transfiguring her by love, then is passion at its sweetest, life at its highest. In this opening gush, or burst, of the 8th Symphony (*allegro vivace e con brio*) we seem to have such love. Here is that rapture we missed in the expressly culled Pastoral Symphony—rapture of emancipation, thrill and burst of joy! The great action of the Eroica, and C minor—aye, and of the A major symphonies— here gives place to the pure ecstatic emotion.

Here we have indeed the broad breath of the fields ; we perfectly revel in the flowery gold ; the sweet streams winding there enchant us ; the blue mountains sublime us with their great tender reminders ; in the divine whole—this "*transcenden Tempel des Frühlings*"—we are ready to fall on our knees for joy. Rural, without doubt, are these opening strains ; "escaped into the country"—"love in the country," seems written over them. Later, Alberti's and Elter- lein's notion (independent) more obtains ; "the symphony represents humour," (chiefly caprice, mood); "the base and character of the work is throughout humouristic." This, however, may well be, and the scene of these caprices still remains the divine country ; the lights and shadows and fleecy clouds of the soul amid those of nature. Here we may fancy the scene of a superior Watteau. By running brook and sway- ing bough, gracious nymph and gallant swain exchange

fancies and glances, and sport, and make love. Nay
it is indeed like a back-glance of our Beethoven himself into his early years—when the days were bluer,
the world broader, by the celestial Rhine yonder, and
when he too, in his sweet and awful heart, felt
shy unutterable emotions; thrill'd, as though fire
had flashed in waves through his veins when *she*
touched his hand—that hand to be so creative. This
may be a glance at those days, as the Countess Guic-
ciardini Sonata (most lyric of all, like the passion of
an Oriental night) is a burning record of others.

In a word, and finally, Beethoven, who was essen
tially imaginative, has in this pendent to the Fourth
Symphony, given himself up to, and given us, fancy;
and a gracious present it is, like a handful of pearls,
from the master. Not less precious, but more precious, are the smiles and sportive caresses of Hercules
—the pleasantries of Jove. Ah ! He who challenged
the terrors of the cross, and threatened *Dies Irae*,
(we must ever recur to Him as our highest type),
spoke of the lilies of the field, and gathered to him
little children; and more precious, if possible, than
his words, or very deeds, were—if He ever had them
—his smiles.

The query is suggested by this youth-fresh work—
did Beethoven write this Opus 93 out of his heart
at that age (if so, what a heart !—with styles one and
three close together), or did he draw upon fancies of
his early years—tone-lyrics of that time ?

The Allegretto Scherzando, that Ariel-gush ("On a
bat's back I do fly") is thus described by the German critic :—"In the second movement we have,
especially, naïve joy ; nay, at once the child-like
innocence and mischievous sport of humour. The
first motiv (as is well known) had its origin in a play-

ful canon improvised by Beethoven for the metro-
nome-maker, Maelzel; the whole piece has been
praised by many, as the most charming morçeaux of
Beethoven's." The Minuet he speaks of as dry
humour, the Trio as revealing an inner *Liebesdrange*
(urgent need of and for love)—such as is ever innate
in the true humourist."

The Finale seems another piece of "Tempest"
music; now grateful as chased or filagree silver, now
inly tender, as the soul of Ferdinand and Miranda of
course is; now, even with a glance at the "dæmonish."
These extraordinary " *Schreckennoten*," now as C sharp,
now as D flat—which we were tempted to substitute on
the first appearance of the note as C sharp—may furnish another pretty quarrel between the wrang'ers over
"False Notation." They form one of the most original flashes of Beethoven (if not a hint of aberration),
and strike us as properly belonging to a profoundly
tragic movement, and not to such a one as this;
where, indeed, their value seems hardly utilised.
Such notes might have been blown as the "Blast
of the breath of His displeasure"—before the Hand-
writing on the Wall; at the Rending of the Veil 'fore
the Holy of Holies; at the dawn of the Day of
Doom; though, indeed, this latter also would break
upon fairy revels, foambells, and butterflies, as well as
wars, earthquakes, and volcanoes.

In conclusion, we regret the absence of an Adagio
in this genial work. We now turn to the portentous
Choral Symphony.

THE CHORAL SYMPHONY, OP. 125.

A noble poet, on reading certain strophes in a long
poem to a friend, remarked that they were experiments. The remark rather jarred, at the time, on the

friend's ear, and sunk into his mind. *Apropos*, say what one will about the Choral Symphony, it strikes us as an experiment. The very title seems empiric. What we should understand by a choral symphony would be a symphonically grand chorus blended with a symphony; but this is rather a chorus preceded by a symphony—its opposite, too (though intentionally), in character; in part independent of, in part made up of the themes of the chorus. Now, a similar work—Mendelssohn's "Lobgesang,"—struck us as being likewise an experiment, and not a happy one; the prevailing and overpowering impression was—"Oh! when will the singers begin?" This gigantic preluding of the essential is a distracting postponement, a colossal interruption—difficult to be done justice to by the impatient hearer, even if perfect in itself. But, if perfect *in* itself, it would be more perfect *by* itself—(?)—for, as a prelude, it remains subordinate; and this to the symphony is fatally derogatory. Most "experiments" are mistakes in judgment, and these in art. This symphony strikes us as disproportionate as well as incongruous —no less serious musical than statuesque and architectural faults. We feel that it is indeed bound up with, but not one of the others; that it is an appendix. Beethoven himself began, after it, another symphony, whole in itself, like the others. No doubt he was impressed (and rightly) with the feeling that an Ode to Joy demanded a grandiose introduction; but he made an elementary mistake (?) in making that introduction too long and heterogeneous—in short, by giving us a symphony instead of an overture. With respect to its character, let us draw a little nearer—it is, no doubt, of the greatest importance. In this symphony, Beethoven summoned

up all his then powers to pour forth and portray
in one tremendous focus *the* conflict wh.ch his
symphonies and deeper music more or less generally depict, viz., that of Pessimism and Optimism—of good and evil.   And in this he was herald-
representative of the nineteenth century.   Bach,
Handel, Haydn, and Mozart, did not depict this
struggle ; at least we are not *struck* by it.   Pathos,
and even tragedy, in general they too of course
reveal—for joy and sadness make up music ; nay,
sadness is perhaps the soul of music, at least Beethoven makes us think so ;   but the characteristic
Hamletism of the nineteenth century (which is Ham
let—as, according to Freiligrath, Germany is, or was
before 1870),—it was reserved for Beethoven to mani
fest forth ; Beethoven, the greatest Hamlet (not Faust
he was too good) of all.   The other centuries were
centuries of belief or unbelief ; this is one of doubt,
with a soul—belief, groping after a new one.   It *wil*
be new, and not local—let alone parochial.   Fearful
doubts must have seized thinking, feeling men, at all
times, after looking abroad and pondering what we
have called this tremendous paradox and discrepancy,
the universe.   St. Paul himself said, with poignant
realization, " The world groaneth and travaileth until
' now ' ;" and it is difficult to overstate the wide-spread
and individual imperfection and unhappiness.   This
sense, of old, drove men into what we called a frenzy-
of belief—in something exterior.   That they clutched,
and to that they clung, nailing their gaze, as it were,
to happiness promised for faith bestowed ; and full of
such a fearful sense of the wretchedness below, that
they laughed to scorn even torture and the stake ;
and warped away from this world, to bide wholly in
the contemplation of another.   As might have been

predicted, however, this, too, could only be a phase and period of transition (and that not a long one in the history of man ; we must revolutionise our ideas of time and greatness) ; and, inevitably, when science, beginning greatly with Copernicus, set in, Luther, the first Freethinker (modern), would soon follow, and in due course a Hume, a Spinoza, a Schopenhauer, and a Kant. Our Beethoven, who had his own "categorical inspiration," no doubt derived terrible arguments for Pessimism from few things more emphatic than his own life—so mysteriously gifted and afflicted, stinted and endowed. Hence, then, the Titanic character of his music ; the tremendous temptation in the wilderness (of his own heart, of a feared to be God abandoned world), of a soul inclining to good, to go over to evil—but the good in the end is triumphant, and we see it ever struggling through :—

> In pits of passion and dens of woe
> We see strong Eros struggling through.

At the end of the awful conflict shadowed forth in the colossal opening of the choral symphony, we have been tempted to inscribe, "as if the world's heartstrings were cracking" :—

—the atheism of a King David himself : "the fool hath said in his heart, there is no God !" but after

that (the recitative to " O'er the raging waters of
Galilee, the voice of One ' who made the storm his
mere mantle, and the sea the pathway of power'" :)
the voice of peace—in modern dialect the voice of
man ; in the light of which reading, this entry of the
human voice becomes portentous, as though it said,
let the elements rage, let the arts stutter, the human
voice alone can bring relief—light, and hope, and
joy.

Thus, Beethoven's design was characteristically and
colossally grand ; he wished to strive to paint what
painting certainly could not, and what sculpture
could not—nay, in a sense, what poetry could not,
for words cannot represent a conflict (especially of
the emotions) like music, cannot so awfully or
sweetly thrill the soul.   And he succeeded in a way
that Michael Angelo (his analogue) and Raphael
(whom Beethoven also blended with the Angelo in
him), certainly did not, when they foolishly attempted
to paint the unpaintable (the Last Judgment, and
Transfiguration).   Whether, however, he succeeded
musically, in this symphony, as a tail-work, is a de-
bateable question.   The query may be put—Might
he not have treated the Pessimism also vocally, and
thereby avoided the undue length and unsupported
character of the instrumental prelude?   The work
would then have been a homogenous whole.   But,
and perhaps even more importantly, the question
arises— Might not the music itself have been better?
The second movement, *Molto vivace,* marvellously
pourtrays (before Wagner) the *Venusberg*—the Me-
phistopheles-pact into which the poor despairing
Pessimist may be driven to plunge ; and we recollect well how we felt after first hearing the *Adagio
molto e cantabile,* and going away perforce into the

outside world; *Ach ! that* is the true world—that world we have been in ; and this is a world of dross ! But the first movement we cannot help feeling to be laboured, especially in parts, compared with that of the C minor, which is simply one rush of inspiration, and the chief theme of the last movement is, we must say it, tame and undignified, if not commonplace—nay, almost "jiggy," played and sung so fast (*allegro assai*) —not to compare for one moment with that other burst, the Hallelujah Chorus, (or "For unto us"), or many of Beethoven's own motivs. But, besides, it is guilty of the gross, the heinous offence in this instance, of setting words utterly different. Here is the melody ; notice, besides its extremely smooth (amounting, as we say, to the commonplace) character (and so, not characteristic)—notice, that it consists (*mirabile dictu !*) merely of one strain repeated, with the cadence slightly altered (full, instead of half) :—

"Joy, thou gracious spark of God, His daughter, out of heaven sped."

" With thy fire intoxicated, we thy sanctuary tread."

it continues--

" Thy blessed magic binds again, Ties sever'd by the world."

and then the phrase to the words " With thy fire intoxicated," &c., is used for :—

> " All men are Brothers, where, sweet Joy,
>   Thy gentle wing is furl'd."

But, much worse—nay, absolutely shocking to the spiritual sense, is the persistent use of the same phrase, mediocre as it is, to these words :—

> " Who that victory hath gained,
>   Of a friend, the friend to be ;
>   Who a graceful wife hath gained

(This, too, should hardly be sung by women ?)

> Mix with ours his ' holy glee' ; *
> Yea, who calls but one soul his
> In all this round of sea and land :
> He who never knew that blessing
> Steal in tears from this bright band."

Would it have been thought possible for Beethoven (Inspired Instinct), to set these last lines to the same —we are almost provoked to say, rattling jingle. To a lower deep, alas ! our Beethoven-Hamlet could scarcely fall—

> " Oh, what a sovereign mind is there o'erthrown !"

It was an incredible aboriginal mistake to set these lines to the same time, let alone same tune. Nor, indeed, can his choice of the words be considered happy. What made him in his grand old age (old for him) so harp upon Schiller's crude performance, we know not ; nay, we ask whether a Beethoven should not have treated the glorious subject, Joy,

---

* Wordsworth's sonnet on the Swiss.

when he was already young;—despise as he might (an egregious error) his earlier works. Had he at least undertaken it when he wrote the Symphony in D and the "Eroica"; or, in the "high and palmy state" of his powers, when he wrote the *facile princeps* C minor! Schiller's first words would alone repel us; he talks—"babbles" would be the strictly truer word, barbarously babbles—of joy, as that spark of the gods, and, in the same breath, daughter out of Elysium. How could he so talk of that grand abstract fact—Joy! Joy, the sunshine of the soul—whose glow, thence outwards, fills the Universe; life, absolute being; wherein alone we rightly, fully live. We have no patience with such barbarous metaphorising, such schoolboy personification, such hectic rapture! No wonder Beethoven failed, falling on such words as these.

(In passing—he has a few bars of interlude which Mendelssohn's famous " 'Tis thus decreed," strangely resembles.)

If the C were sharp, the passages would be identical.

In continuation—Beethoven seems in general equally careless (or perverse) and unhappy in his treatment of the words—a curious misfortune in an expressly vocal celebration. We have the same smooth passages, and the same rattling pace, for various inflections of thought and feeling. He does not fail, however, to give us one of those "flashes" of

his true genius, old power, which Spohr alluded to,
at the words *ver Gott* :—

He proceeds thenceforth to intermix symphony
with words in the way we spoke of as that which
would seem natural to a choral symphony ; and of
the passage where the great broad theme (far happier)
is *blended* below, with the original motiv.   Dr. Nohl
strikingly remarks, that " Lo ! here was a proof that
music is also a thinker !"   No doubt in our glorious
Beethoven, who was all heart, and soul, and brain,
(*plus* robust body, till his sad latter days), if not
exactly *mens sana in corpore sano.*

Nevertheless, on the whole, we feel we must agree
with Spohr (surely no unworthy judge, unless blinded
by envy) ; and still rank this symphony as a colossal
experiment rather than a genial success.   As far as
our feelings are a guide (and we have expressly
acknowledged at the outset, how each one of us is
the creature of prejudice and mood), we find the
work veritably stamped and distinguished by laboured
elaboration—nay, almost painful labour.   Beethoven
(we feel) perpetuated a fundamental, primary, pregnant mistake, in *setting himself* to " work out " one
melodic idea, and that such a poor one—disappoint-
ing almost to exasperation.   Above all, varied words
cannot be so set.   Even in purely instrumental music
the possibility soon has its natural limits, whatever
the genius of the composer, and despite the unde-
niably great effects that may be accomplished.   Did

not Beethoven himself, on overhearing his—how many variations was it, on a theme?—exclaim: "Oh, Beethoven, what an ass thou art!" There spoke the great man! Nature will never be sacrificed to a crotchet.

The design of this celebrated work was grand, characteristic, worthy of its great designer; but the execution we cannot feel corresponded. It seems to us the A-B-C of reasoning, that a time *must* come in the career of every man when his powers decay. We speak, and rightly, of the records of his brain as messages from the Infinite; but, nevertheless, when those cells get enfeebled, that telegraph of nervous tissue corrupted, the messages are no longer mighty as of yore: Divine messages do not and will not come, except through the mystically-operating (for they also are divine) healthy physical mediums. Psychology and physiology are inextricably blended, if not one. Beethoven's faculties, then, it seems to us, had already begun to decay—he was older than other men at his years. He had been long deaf; was almost broken down with worry and care; and, probably, alas! trembled on the verge of incipient insanity (were it not already incipient). He was no longer rich in the fresh originality of his prime—in the original freshness of his youth; he had, perhaps, essentially written himself out (herein below Shakespeare). He began to repeat himself, to theorise, to *make* music. Did he not himself say, "I plan, but when I sit down to perform, I find I have nothing to write." There again spoke the truly great man, honest to the last. He could, of course, never get away from his individuality—get out of himself; no man can. But even ideas now seemed to fail him, and their absence is no compensation for a new style of the old individual, let alone when that is dubious.

To sum up.   The Choral Symphony seems, at the best, a grand but doubtful experiment. Its greatest, its only inspired movement, is the adagio ; and that, heavenly as it is, interferes with the progress of the work—with the scheme of it—as depicting doubt, denial, and despair ("there shall be wailing and gnashing of teeth"), to be followed by oil upon the waters—by an uncontrollable outburst, sacred fury almost, of joy, at the perception by man that he is imperishable, part of the All ; not only recipient of joy here, but justified demander and mortgagee of it hereafter ; and joy of joy even at the high perception that even if we personally are not immortal, we are bubbles of the eternal sea, and that is immortal.

Summing Up.

Finally, it is such thoughts as these, consciously or unconsciously expressed, which stamp and distinguish Beethoven's music as a whole, to which we now turn. In his jubilation is the "fulness of joy"; in his sadness the core of sorrow. He has "made the passage from heaven to hell"; he has sounded the gamut of sound. In his four great symphonies, the one in D (the rushing forth and soaring up of youth, Elterlein considers it) ; the Eroica, the C minor, and the A major ; in these four symphonies, to which the soul's eye in predilection turns, which stand out from all the rest ; and in many of his other works— whose soul is as great, but substance less—we see Beethoven, probably the most glorious emotional representative of man in history—not only in music, but art, almost literature. He is thus the greatest phenomenon perhaps of modern times after Shakespeare. Shakespeare over-tops him; but who else? Not Dante—too fierce, and crude, and narrow (see how blatant he is about Mahomet, and his annotator, Professor Bianchi, ten times worse—he has the most stupendously stupid note we ever read!) not Milton, less rich and influential; not his own contemporary and countryman, Goethe, whose Faust and Egmont are in Beethoven's music rather than in his own words, and who had not Beethoven's genial humanity, world-wide breadth, heaven's-heart depth, and titanic power. Only his Fatherland's philosophical giants, methinks, can rank with him; and their influence and effect are naturally limited. He thought in music— the most delicious volumes of philosophy! thought and feeling are presented to us in one—aye, and painting too. *Apropos,* so also do we rank him above the artists. The works of Apelles and Phidias are gone; the very Parthenon is going. But his works will last; and they mesmerise and master us with a power which theirs never could do—theirs, and Angelo's, and Raphael's; or Rubens, and Rembrandt, and Turner. For music is the highest of the arts, as being most the message of the Highest: and here is the music of the highest of her messengers. Yes! for only Handel (whom he so characteristically revered) can match with him, and that only in power. In originality, in richness, in depth (including intensity —glow), in humanity, eminently in influence think) of Beethoven's sonatas spread over the world, besides his quartets and symphonies, pyramidal models; whereas Handel would hardly be known but for his "Messiah," and that chiefly in England); in a word, in universality, and a certain mystical soul of meaning—sacred mystery of insight and sorrow—within

him; in these he surpasses Handel—and all. Not
that he has exhausted music. No. Music was considered exhausted before him; and even his music,
symphonies and sonatas alike, are of unequal quality
and merit individually as well as comparatively.
And not that all great music does not, more or less,
like his work—reveal (or shadow forth) what his
does; and instrumentation has made advances since
him; but he is the *ne plus ultra* as yet, though not,
indeed, without companions. For this is a law as
much morally or intellectually as physically. The
highest peaks in the Himalayas, Andes, and Alps,
are together; and here the appearances around me
preach the same truth. One summit is the special
manifestation of a general upheaval (we have already
given particular instances), and these take place at
periods. The musical upheaval (the tertiary deposit)
has taken place late. Primevally was the architectural (least original, and slowest of all the arts—?),
then the sculptural, pictorial, and poetic; groups and
series, peaks and summits of masters, in all. With
revived art and literature came the quasi seraph,
Shakespeare; then science and music, contemporary
with the greatest movement in philosophy, and this
significantly—for nothing happens without import
and relation. Beethoven, it is true, set masses; but
he was essentially a Theist, if not Pantheist (unconscious pantheism, we take it, is the soul of his music).
One worthy gentleman delivered himself of the following lucubration *re* Beethoven's "Mount of
Olives":—"It is a fine work, *but* proves its author to
have been a Deist, and—" Oh, that "but"! I cry
you mercy, my fine particle; there is great virtue too
in a "but." We could not help smiling, and thinking of "Poor God, with nobody to help him!"

A highly curious and most instructive fact about Beethoven is, that (as we before remarked, I think), it is very difficult, if not impossible, to find his analogue. In this individuality he is sublime. Hardly any comparison satisfies us; neither Aiskulos, Homer, Virgil, Dante, Milton, or Shakespeare, is exactly his like. He has Dante's intensity, Milton's sublimity (more organ-like than Dante's), and Shakespeare's universality to a great extent — that is, his humanity and quasi superhuman lyrical beauty and dramatic power, but not his wonderful comic genius (as far as we can judge from music, though Beethoven's shows undoubted humour—which is part, indeed, of humanity) ; his *characteristic*, seraphic serenity, and infinity, wealth of creation, and inexhaustibility to the last. Beethoven is a unique (as Carlyle called Dickens) blending of these three (and allied to Shakespeare most), *plus* his own great indispensable self (for there is ever a new factor in every new man). Neither can we quite match him with any of the artists. He has the severity of Phidias — or Praxiteles—who was famous for bronze, the grandeur of Bruneleschi and Angelo, the grace and feeling of Raffael and Canova, the mystic splendour of Turner, and the unique originality, the powerful chiaroscuro of Rembrandt. Indeed, his relationship to the latter is curiously interesting. These words, applied to Rembrandt, might be applied to Beethoven :—" His advance from youth to age is marked, if not by inexperience or feebleness, at all events by successive and distinctive manners." "The product of his art is startling; it is singular for individuality of character, supreme in light, shade, and colour." Beethoven, however, was not an "artist who took what may be termed his daily constitutional walk through the lower types of nature;" rather he was a Jove's eagle, a Gannymede on his pinions, winging his unseen way through empyreans. Among the artists of his own vocation he is likewise unique. It is true, that as Guinicelli closely preceded Dante (and may even be called his master—*Il Saggio* Dante names him); as Tasso, and Ariosto, and Shakespeare, and Milton, were a grand cluster in the Elizabethan period, Corneille, Racine, and Voltaire later, Schiller, Goethe, and Wieland, after; so Beethoven splendours in what we have called the Orion's Belt of music, Haydn, Mozart, and Beethoven; but, to slightly vary, he is the red star in Orion, the Mont Blanc of the Alps; neither is Handel, the great sun in the " constellation Hercules " (to which our system is said to move), his superior—or quite his equal.

Our persuasion of Beethoven's religious impressions (" he could be seldom got to speak about religion ") was derived rather from internal evidence : but here is an explicit passage on the matter. We read in his *Tagebuch*, 1816, underlined, and written out in his own hand :—" *Aus der Indischen Literatur :* God is immaterial, therefore unthinkable : (*geht über jeden Begriff:* since he is invisible, he can have no form). But, from what we can gather in his works, we may conclude that He is almighty, all-knowing, and omni-present." The following (still more significant) he wrote out in a *Quartblatt*, in large letters, had framed, and kept before him on his writing-table. It was taken from the temple of the Egyptian goddess, Neith, at Sais :—

1. I Am what Is.

2. I am all that is, was, will be.   No mortal hath ever lifted my veil.

3. He is alone, self existent (*Er ist allein von ihm selbst*); and to this Unique all things owe their being.

In the last sentence, we may observe, there is (as usual) a contradiction with the first—a confusion between theism and pantheism; for, if the great I Am *is* all, all things cannot be said to owe their being to him, but *are* him—fragmentary manifestations of him.

A list of the books found in Beethoven's *Hand-bibliothck*, are also, in some sort, a key to the man (and his music). *Ecco!* Shakespeare; Goethe's Poems, "Wilhelm Meister," and "Faust"; Schiller; Tiedge's "Urania" (Beethoven's beautiful "An die Hoffnung," Op. 32, is a setting of a song in that); Seumes' and Matthison's Poems, and others; "Briefe an Natalie über Gesang," von Nina d'Aubigny-Engelbrunner (much esteemed, and recommended by Beethoven); Klopstock; Zach; Werner; Herder (Goethe's "Master"); Plato; Aristotle; Xenophon; Plutarch; Euripides; Horace; Pliny; Quintilian (these, I presume, translated—Dr. Nohl does not say); Thomson (whose nature-painting made him specially prized); and Ossian (Napoleon's favourite).

We read that against the words, often cited too, of Carlyle, "Two things strike me dumb; the moral law within us, and the starry heavens over us"; he wrote — " *mit kräftigen Schrift-zug*"— KANT. In his celebrated will, we read —"I will seize Fate by the throat, quite bow me down it never shall." In his Journal, 1816, we read, "The grand mark of a great man; stedfastness in unhappy circumstances." One of his remarks was this :—"There is nothing higher than this—to get

nearer to the Godhead than other men ; and thence
diffuse its beams over mankind." Another noteworthy observation was this :—" Celebrated artists
are always prejudiced (or pre-occupied) ; therefore, their first works are the best, although they
germinated in obscurity."—(Nohl's "Life of Beethoven," vol. 3, p. 238). One of his most pregnant
remarks was the following :—"All real invention is
moral progress" (*Alle echte Erfindung ist moralisher
Fortschritt*).

Beethoven's music is so pregnant, that it is difficult
to sum up what it contains. As before stated, it is a
microcosm, both of man and the world : it especially
unrolls before us man (how he thinks, and feels, and
fights) as much as the powerful disquisitions of a
Kant or Hegel. It is representative, because so intensely subjective ; representative from himself outward—he being not a narrowly but comprehensively
subjective soul ; we find in it (very profoundly) his
own unsatisfied heart—type of how much in the
world ! We find in it his unhappy life—type of still
more. We find in it his intense character, full of
sublime passion, and only more dear to us for its
faults. We find in it his infirmities—especially a
dark prophesy of *mens* INSANA *in corpore insano;* but
we were spared that sad spectacle, by the "cruel-to-
be-kind" messenger of Providence. We find in it
the pure passionate love of Nature most concentrated
in the Teutonic nature—coruscating with mystic
sparks shooting from the heart on all sides outward.
We find in it at once the most intense lyrical and
dramatic power hitherto known. We find in it, alike,
gracious fancy and grand imagination. We find in it
humanity and humour. Moreover, we find in it the
grandest *objective* power of painting—heroic battles,

as well as with hope—on "our prison walls; far-reaching landscapes and aurora"; together with a subjective power and pre-eminence that is almost awful in its majesty. We find in it the subtle and the sublime—if it be not for sublime to be subtle. Last, and lowest, we find in it unsettled faith—distracting a soul of good, wearying and worrying his great good heart, but not overcoming it:

> "It could not bring him wholly under more
> Than loud south-westerns, rolling ridge on ridge
> The buoy that rides at sea, and dips and springs
> For ever;"

and herein is our Beethoven—he, too, a man of sorrows, and acquainted with grief. *Ach!* Man is that, most—most intensely representative. This is the real reason why he so speaks to us, and shakes us; why he so influenced his contemporaries and followers. An age is represented by its greatest—that is, by the richest in goodness and insight, and these mutually represent each other; but you will not find them in temple or tabernacle—except, indeed, that not made by hands. You will find them where you find their heart—(where a man's treasure is, there is his heart also). Ask them what they think, and feel. You will find that they consider all our common *isms* and *alities* but as episodes—aye, and brief ones—if not, more or less, unconscious insanities. That, inevitably, as the world in its giant history proceeded from Nothingism (for how many ages?) to Fetishism—to Confuciusism—to Buddhism—to Jewism—to Paganism (or Greek and Romanism)—to Christianity; so common Christianity (the temporal, dogmatic, superstitious, local, parochial), must also proceed to something higher; which shall be at once

outcome and all-compriser of the rest.   Man has got
to realise his identity with the Imperishable (caring
little, if he must "soon be making head to go" from
this—has soon "notice to quit" this lodging—in the
cold ground);   the absolute indestructibility of any
one manifestation of force—or rather fact of force—
for the manifestations change, and pass away.   He
has got to learn to love goodness for its own sake
alone, and know that Conscience is God—*realising*
with the most lyric and scientific conviction that *every*
violation of right or law, moral even more inevitably
than physical—let every one search his own life and
conscience for the proof—is punished here without
or within—frequently, and most sublimely, subtly,
within.   Finally, he has got to make this his faith
that—while clinging to the truly blessed hope of
everlasting life, which is the natural corollary of our
consciousness, as our dearest sheet-anchor; as the
sense that most makes us feel infinite; and as the
soul of beauty, or beautifying soul of all—so, nevertheless, the practical immortality of right action (or of
goodness) perpetuating itself in what we do and say,
here and now—is our chief concern, the sole thing
essential; which we may supplement and consum-
mate by falling back on the tremendous realization
before expressed.   If *we* are not immortal, we are
bubbles of the eternal sea of being, and *that* is——

Once again, then, let us repeat, such high belief,
more or less, is the *soul* of Beethoven's music (aye,
even in his masses, for the eternal speaks behind the
temporary, the mask; hence its specific gravity
(greatest of all), its infinite significance.   He is the
morning star of this reformation, the breast-inflaming
dawn of a new heaven in a grander clime—new firma
ment over New Jerusalem.   Powdered-wigged Haydn

and Mozart—powdered-wigged genius even, including full-bottomed-wigged Handel—could not proclaim such a creed;—almost, as it were, with thunder of cannon. But Beethoven ushered in the nineteenth century; he was the Napoleon of its better half—highei life; and in due time and order followers and apostles will succeed—have already arisen. The symphony, especially the un-betitled be-programmed symphony, is the purest manifestation of music, whose eloquence is better than words—(space, too, is silent); and the talk of sundry German professors, &c., about music "no longer playing a single part," coolly assuming, almost, the symphony to be an exploded error, we are almost tempted to describe as crotchety maundering or wordy wind, if not blatant jargon. This superfluous pity for music standing alone, also reminds us of " Poor God ! with nobody to help him !" No ! the symphony will still be penned by the tone-poet—inte ,sely feeling and thinking, lyrico-dramatic man. It will be broad as the world, and have a soul of the highest. It will be the grandest absolute expression of the best which we see and are. But it will also be counterparted and supplemented by the " Word-made-Flesh " in tone (the Word is never so beautifully made Flesh as in tone), as Thought is made Flesh in the Word. Religion is the Heart of Art, whence all pulses and flows ; and composers will—at last—get sick of setting twaddle and dogma, however venerable; and will celebrate pure truth, old or new. In setting the Higher Utterance of the past, they will reject the husk and keep the kernel—that of eternal universal application ; or they will transfigure by ideal interpretation. In setting the new, they will set lyrical expression of the profound poet—the earnest words of the intense thinker, and not the jingle of the song-writer, the farrago of the libretto-concocter. In a word, the higher oratorio (as well as the higher drama), will play its part; be the exponent—as the symphony will be the expression—of the new man. This will be the mightiest manifestation of music—universal truth, profound feeling, transcendency, and humanity; Shakespeare and Emerson (not Milton) in one; incarnate in tone, published and borne aloft by Music and the Human Voice; culminating in such apotheosis at last!—after so many ages of stuttering, *singing* will at length have reached to Highest Thought!

THE END.

www.ingramcontent.com/pod-product-compliance
Lightning Source LLC
Chambersburg PA
CBHW020411030726
47496CB00007B/2410